Praise for *Up High in the Trees:*

"Brinkman has chosen the perfect story for a debut. With a mother's patience, she brings Sebby step-by-step back into the world of the living."
—Susan Salter Reynolds, *Los Angeles Times*

"[A] luminous—and ultimately uplifting—debut novel."
—Linda Fears, *Parents*

"A very beautiful and deeply strange little book."
—Suzanne Kleid, KQED *Arts & Literature*

"This is an astonishing debut by a gifted young writer. *Up High in the Trees* captures, pitch-perfectly, the voice of one eight-year-old boy. That the story is also compelling, beautifully written, humorous, and heartbreaking makes it necessary reading. Sebby Lane is a Little Prince for our times."
—Cristina Garcia, author of *Dreaming in Cuban*

"[Brinkman has the] impressive ability to connect with and portray the myopic grief of a bereft child."
—*Kirkus Reviews*

"*Up High in the Trees* is a beautiful—and fearless—book. In Sebby, Kiara Brinkman has created an indelible character whose voice is at once lyrical and absolutely real. A haunting, deeply moving work by a shockingly talented new writer."
—Katharine Noel, author of *Halfway House*

"A very moving and perfectly convincing evocation of the inner life of an unusual boy. . . . Brinkman's portrait of Sebby and his family is humane and uncompromising, never maudlin, and, in the end, we root for Sebby as if he were our own."
—Dave Eggers, author of *What Is the What*

"An achingly beautiful story . . . The surprise in this novel is the assured talent of such a young writer and the wisdom of such a little boy."
—Mary Jo Anderson, *The Chronicle Herald* (Canada)

"[A] sincere, sober debut . . . Told in brief, poetic vignettes, the novel moves quickly and episodically, like a series of snapshots from the camera of Sebby's unique mind."
—*Publishers Weekly*

"The real gem of this novel [is] Sebby's somewhat robotic, distant voice that lingers long after the book ends."
—Rachel Aydt, *Quest*

"*Up High in the Trees* is a hauntingly beautiful debut, a stunner. Kiara Brinkman has masterfully created an enchanting, poignant, and wholly original child narrator out of taut, spooky, electric sentences and elegant, musical concisions. . . . [A] riveting, often terrifying, depiction of the other-world that is childhood."
—Maud Casey, author of *The Shape of Things to Come*

"A quiet book, often poetic and moving . . . Touching."
—Elizabeth Gold, *San Francisco Chronicle*

"A visceral, heart-wrenching, gorgeous book. What moves me most about Brinkman's first novel is the voice: it's pitch-perfect and mesmerizing. With *Up High in the Trees*, Brinkman has created a fully realized, wholly original, and powerfully felt world."
—Alison Smith, author of *Name All the Animals*

UP HIGH IN THE TREES

UP HIGH IN THE TREES

A Novel

Kiara Brinkman

Grove Press / New York

Published simultaneously in Canada
Printed in the United States of America

FIRST PAPERBACK EDITION

Library of Congress Cataloging-in-Publication Data

Brinkman, Kiara.
Up high in the trees / Kiara Brinkman.
p. cm.
ISBN-13: 978-0-8021-4370-9
ISBN-10: 0-8021-4370-9
1. Mothers and sons—Fiction.   2. Grief—Fiction.
3. Loss (Psychology)—Fiction.   4. Dreams—Fiction.   I. Title.
PS3602.R53185U6 2007
813'.6—dc22   2006052161

Grove Press
an imprint of Grove/Atlantic, Inc.
841 Broadway
New York, NY 10003

Distributed by Publishers Group West

www.groveatlantic.com

08 09 10 11 12   10 9 8 7 6 5 4 3 2 1

for my family

ACCIDENTS

Here it is in my head, right in the place where I keep feeling it and knowing it. Dad knocks on my head like my head is a door. He knocks softly because Dad has big, soft hands. He says my name, Sebby.

Sebby, he says, earth to Sebby.

I come back then, but the things I know stay stuck where they are and I keep knowing them. Dad picks me up and lifts me high so I can reach into the leaves of our tree. Dad tries to hold me up for a long time. His face turns red and a deep sound comes out of his throat, because I'm getting bigger and Dad isn't so strong. He puts me down.

What is it? Dad asks.

I shrug my shoulders to say, Dad, I don't know, so he'll think that it's all gone now. But it's here in my head, in the dark place where you hold things and carry them around.

One thing I know is that I'm going to live for a very, very long time.

Mother liked to run in the middle of the night.

She'd wake me up and ask if I wanted to go with her. I nodded, yes. My eyes were sticky. I had to blink a lot to make them stay open.

I held Mother's hand and we walked to the garage. She put me in my old blue stroller that smelled dirty and cold, like how the garage smelled. I was too big, but I could still fit.

Mother pushed me in fast circles around the block. The houses were dark and quiet. Nothing was moving except for us and we were going so fast.

It rained one time and we stopped under a tree.

The rain dripped off the leaves in big, slow drops.

Are you okay? Mother asked.

I nodded, yes. The rain made my stroller smell dirtier and older. Mother took off her T-shirt and her shorts. Mother was soft white like the glass on a frosty white lightbulb. The rain made her shine.

It feels nice, Mother said. She pushed my stroller and we went fast.

I liked how her feet sounded—tap, tap, tap—clean on the wet sidewalk.

I need to sleep, because my head hurts in the dark spots behind my eyes.

Sebastian, Teacher says.

I can hear Teacher's feet click-walking closer to me. Click,
click, click, closer. She puts her hand on my arm.

Are you okay, Sebastian? Teacher asks.

Behind me, Ryan pinches my back.

Ouch, I say.

The kids are laughing. Katya looks at me. She is my friend.

You're okay, Teacher tells me.

I close my eyes and Teacher lets me sleep.

The bell's ringing wakes me up. It's the end of the day and
everyone's lined up at the door. They push each other outside
and run. I stand up to go.

Wait, Teacher says and makes her mouth smile.

She folds a piece of paper and tells me it's a note to give
to Dad. I take it from her.

Okay, bye, I say and leave.

I walk until I'm outside of school and then stop to unfold
the paper. The note says:

Dear Mr. Lane,

    I'm worried that Sebastian may not be getting a full
night of sleep at home. Recently, he's been dozing off
in class. I've also noticed him squinting and rubbing his

eyes—maybe he needs glasses? As you know, I am so pleased to have Sebastian in my class—I just want to ensure that he's getting as much as possible out of his school day. Please call me so we can discuss this.

Thank you, Judy Lambert

I don't want Dad to read the note, so I rip it up and then I let go. The pieces blow all around. They sound like leaves on the sidewalk.

A long time ago, Mother let her papers go in the rainstorm. I followed her outside.

She said, Go back in, you'll get yourself sick again.

I went in and watched her from the window. She ripped up her papers and let them fly in the wind. When she came back inside, her face was so white and her eyes were staring off far away, not seeing anything.

All your poems, Dad said to her.

Mother said, Sebby, I'm lonely, come sit with me.

So I sat with her and hid my face in her hair. I wanted to bite her because she smelled so good.

The rain stopped and we went out to look. Little wet papers were stuck onto the house. Dad said to help, so I helped Dad peel them off. We found one with a whole word that didn't get washed off by the rain and Dad said to put it in my pocket, because it was for me.

What does it say? I asked.

Dad said the word said baby.

I want to be home now. The ripped-up note from Teacher is flying all around me. I run away from the note.

At home, the door is unlocked.

Sebby, that you? my brother's voice asks from the kitchen.

It's me, I say. My forehead is sweating. The inside air feels cold on my face. I go to the kitchen and there's Leo, eating pickles.

What'd you do, run all the way home? he asks.

I don't say anything. Leo tells me he has to go to the library.

Do you want to come with? he asks. Leo's in eleventh grade and he's in smart classes at his school because he reads so much. He can read a whole book with chapters in two hours. I like to watch his eyes moving back and forth, back and forth over the pages.

I can't tell him about the note from Teacher. The note is a secret. Now I know it was not right to rip it up because Ms. Lambert is a good teacher to me. She lets me go outside and breathe the air by myself when I need to. I like it when she comes close to look at my work and her brown-black hair touches the top of my desk and her smell is like the Chap Stick she puts on her lips.

I follow Leo to the library. I walk behind him so I can step in the same places he steps. Leo doesn't like it when I do this. He stops still all of a sudden and makes me bump into his back.

Cut it out, he says.

The library has so many books you can smell the sour smell of the pages getting old. Leo takes out all his folders and his pencil pouch. He puts up his arms and reaches as high as he can because that makes him feel ready to work. The ceiling is far away and Leo's happy because there's space for stretching and thinking. I tap him on the shoulder.

Not now, Sebby, he says, I have to study for my chemistry test.

I slide down off my chair and go under the table where it's dark. My eyes are hurting. There's too much time and I want to fall asleep, so I close my eyes, but I can't sleep, because I have a question in my head. The air is quiet. I open my eyes and watch my brother's foot tapping.

Then I crawl back up onto my chair and sit next to him. He doesn't look at me, so I write down my question in big letters at the top of one of his papers and I push it in front of him.

Who told you that? he asks me.

I don't say anything.

You don't look like a girl, he says, you need a haircut is all.

Okay, I say. I stand up and push in my chair.

Where are you going? he asks.

I shrug.

Just don't hide from me again, he says.

Okay, I say.

I liked to sit in the cabinet under the sink.

Dad said, I don't understand why you hide under there.

I hugged my knees tight to make myself smaller.

If you sit under there like that for too long, you'll stop growing, Dad said.

Stop it, Mother told him.

They got mad at each other then and I held very still.

Under the sink was the dirty smell, like cooked carrots. It's true that carrots grow down instead of up. I thought of growing down into the ground, deeper and deeper, and I knew then that the whole inside of the earth smelled like dirty carrots.

If he wants to hide, Mother said, let him hide.

Dad said, It's not normal. Dad's voice was loud and mean.

Why are you so worried about what's normal? Mother asked. Her voice was louder now, too.

Louise, Dad said and he put up both of his hands, like two stop signs.

You're not worried about him, she yelled, you're worried about what's normal.

Just tell me why you're so mad, will you? Dad asked.

I can't, Mother said. I'm leaving, she said and then she left.

Downstairs in the library, the books reach all the way to the ceiling. You have to climb up a ladder to touch the highest ones. I don't like how there are so many books. I don't know which one to pick out and read so I don't read any of them. I put my face up close to the pages and they smell peppery, like how the wood floor smells at home.

I walk until I find the right spot. At the very top, one shelf has a long empty space. I climb up the ladder to the empty space and make myself fit. I have to lie on my side because when I lie on my back, it feels like I'm going to fall off.

Leo said not to hide.

In the quiet you can tell when you are doing something wrong, because the quiet gets more quiet. I try to hold very still. I think about how nobody's seeing me and nobody's hearing me and then I can pretend to be not here at all. But the shelf is hard and I can feel my body against the shelf and I know I am here.

Leo said not to hide, so I climb down the ladder.

To make the time go by, I look at all the reading posters on the wall. President George Bush reading, and Bill and Ted, from the movie *Bill and Ted's Excellent Adventure,* both reading and trying to make their faces look smart. My favorite is the one with the kittens climbing around on a pile of books. You can tell the kitten poster is old because it has yellow, turned-up corners and rips fixed with tape.

Upstairs, I go stand by Leo. He looks at me and nods, but doesn't say anything because he's in the middle of thinking about something. If he talks, then he loses what he's thinking about and gets mad. I crawl under the table and watch his foot tap. I press my ear against the floor and I can feel the tapping in the back of my head.

Why's he asleep down there? says my sister's voice. She sometimes comes with the car to give us a ride home.

I'm not asleep, I say with my eyes closed.

Why're you lying on your back like a dead man? she asks me. Why's he lying like that? she asks Leo. It's creepy, she says.

I open my eyes and Leo is bent over, looking down at me.

Why didn't you tell him to stop doing that? she asks him.

I'm not doing anything, I say.

Leo laughs at me. My sister stares hard at his face and then walks away.

Cass, Leo calls in a voice that's half-loud and half whisper, because the rule in the library is that you have to be quiet.

Cass keeps walking away.

Cass, he calls. He says her name again and that makes it sound funny, like it's someone else's name and not a name I know.

I say her name in my head, Cass, Cass, Cass.

Mother named my sister after Mama Cass because Mama Cass had such a sweet voice it could lift you right up off the floor and carry you away. That's what Mother said. Mother showed me a picture of Mama Cass singing alone on a dark stage. In the picture Mama Cass is wearing a long red dress that looks big and full like a red balloon.

I crawl out from under the table and watch Leo put all his papers into different colored folders. Then he puts the folders and books into his red backpack, and that makes his backpack so full, it's hard to zip closed.

We go to the parking lot, but Cass and the green car are gone.

Shit, Leo says.

The way home has a big hill. Leo starts walking fast because he's so mad that he can walk fast even with his heavy backpack. I try to walk fast too, but I'm tired now. I hold on to Leo's coat and practice walking with my eyes closed.

Stop pulling on me, Leo says when we get to the hill, so I let go.

I can still walk with my eyes closed. I listen to Leo's steps on the sidewalk and I copy them.

Our feet make a crunching sound when we get to our gravelly driveway. I open my eyes. Leo kicks up the gravel rocks. He looks tall and angry now and his breathing is fast.

Just go in and leave me alone, Leo says. He throws his backpack against the house and the house makes no sound.

I wait for a sound, but the house is like a giant pillow. Damn you, Leo screams at the house. He goes and picks up his backpack where it landed in Mother's garden.

We had fat, ripe tomatoes. There's a picture in Dad's office of Leo and Cass sitting on a yellow chair, holding Mother's tomatoes. It's like the really old pictures with nobody smiling. The tomatoes are big and round like empty faces.

Dad said I used to eat Mother's tomatoes just like they were apples. He said it made Mother happy to watch me eat.

Dad said, You know, it was hard to make Mother happy. I didn't know that.

When I was little, I practiced drawing different kinds of faces.

Mother sang a song for me:

This is happy
This is sad
This is scared
This is mad.

She made her face match the words.

Leo's mad at the house. He doesn't want to go inside, so I walk to the door by myself. Dad's music is there on the front porch. I can hear his voice singing. Dad gets loud when he sings. I open the door and all the music inside jumps out. It sounds like this: *Goodbye to Rosie*. I know how the Rosie in the song looks. She's blue like how the ghost lady looks on the cover of one of Mother's records. Dad says the blue lady is Joni Mitchell. We don't listen to her record, though, because her voice gives Dad the goose bumps.

Dad's sitting cross-legged on the floor, facing the speakers, so he can't see me. I reach out and touch the back of his neck with one finger. He turns around fast.

Jesus Christ, Sebby, don't do that, Dad says. He grabs my hands and rubs them between his hands. Your hands are freezing, he says.

Cass comes and turns down the music.

Where's Leo? she asks me.

Outside, I say.

What's going on? Dad asks.

Nothing, Cass says.

Dad looks at me and I don't say anything.

Let him stay outside, Cass says.

Dad goes to the door.

Just leave him alone, Cass shouts.

But Dad goes out. He closes the door slowly so it doesn't make any noise.

We're going to eat, Cass says to me.

She takes my hand and pulls me into the kitchen. The table is already set with the brown place mats that have orange and yellow and red leaves on them. Cass pushes down hard on my shoulders to make me sit.

Here, she says.

Cass puts a plateful of steaming spaghetti down on my place mat. I lean forward and let the steam make my face sweaty wet.

Stop it, Cass says. She sits down next to me and uses my knife and fork to cut up the spaghetti.

Dad treats everyone like a baby, Cass says and leans back in her chair. I hear the front door open and then close. There are steps, but Leo and Dad don't come to the kitchen to eat. I look down at my spaghetti because I don't want to see Cass.

Eat, Cass tells me.

It's too hot, I say.

Cass takes a bite of my spaghetti with her fork.

It's fine, she says.

I try a bite.

See, Cass says, it's fine.

She takes another bite and then it's my turn again. We keep taking turns.

How was school? Cass asks.

Long, I tell her.

Cass doesn't have to go to school anymore because she finished twelfth grade and had a graduation. I'm in third, so that means I have nine more grades.

Cass takes another bite and then says, Stop. Stop eating, she says, it doesn't taste right. She gets up and carries the plate over to the sink, then dumps off all the spaghetti.

I stand up and watch her.

Go take a bath, she says.

I don't move. I don't want to take a bath.

I'm tired, I say.

Cass turns off the water. She doesn't look at me.

Whatever, she says, then go to sleep.

I go upstairs and sit down on the top step. If I go to sleep now, then morning will come and I'll have to go back to school. I don't want to go to school, I'll say, and Cass will say there's nowhere else for me to go. In my head, the song says, *Goodbye to Rosie*. I look at the white wall until it makes my eyes go blurry. There are bright spots where Mother touched that haven't been touched by anybody else. You have to look for a long time before you can see a bright spot. Then the spot glows and that's how you know where Mother still is. The spot glows and it's like the spot is glowing inside of you, because it makes you warm inside your chest and that feels good. You want to touch the spot, but you can't because then it will be gone. What's wrong is that everybody always goes around touching everything and Cass is always cleaning and that erases the spots.

I know that when I was three, I was standing on the couch looking out the window at all the flowers. The window was open so I pushed myself out and fell two stories. I landed on my back in Grandmother Bernie's summer garden.

Mother put her hand on her chest and screamed. She could feel her heart in her chest. Her heart felt like it was getting bigger. She kept screaming and ran down the stairs, out the door to me.

I was quiet there in the dirt. Mother picked me up and held me tight. Then I started screaming, too.

Dad was watching from the upstairs window. He ran down to me and Mother. Dad looked at the ground and saw how my head left a dent in the soil. He bent down and kissed the dent. Then he blew a kiss up to Grandmother Bernie and everybody watching us and he couldn't stop blowing kisses because Grandmother Bernie had just put the new garden there with fresh, soft dirt.

Mother held me and she screamed louder and louder— louder than me. Dad put his hands over his ears. I stopped crying and I listened. I could hear everything inside of her.

I didn't talk until after I fell.

Dad tried to get me to talk before that. He sang me songs. He carried me around the house and pointed at everything we saw and told me what it was. He put the words in my head.

Dad took me to the doctor, but Mother wouldn't listen to what the doctor said about me. Mother said I would talk as soon as I had something to say.

After I fell, I said a whole sentence. I want a garden, I told Mother.

Of course, she said.

I helped her plant the seeds. I liked watching all the different colors grow.

Sebby, says Cass's voice.

I can hear her, but I don't want to wake up. She pushes back the hair on my forehead and holds her hand there. Her hand feels cold and then warmer.

Sebby, she says again. She leans in close to me and I can smell her morning pancake-and-syrup smell. She takes her hand off my forehead and it leaves a cold spot.

I stretch my arms up out of the covers. It's morning and I don't want to go to school. My eyes are foggy. I have to rub them so I can see better.

Don't, Cass says, and she pulls my hands down away from my face.

My eyes hurt, I tell her.

That's because you're rubbing them, she says. She's getting my clothes out for me, stacking everything in a neat pile at the bottom of my bed. First my pants, then my shirt, and then my underwear and socks on top. It has to be in this order or else I don't want to get dressed.

How about no school today? she asks.

I nod.

Good, she says, you get ready and I'll call and tell them you're not coming.

My eyes are still foggy. I look out the window and the hill with the big house on top is barely there at all. It's like the outside has gotten smaller. I close my eyes.

Sebby, Cass calls from downstairs.

I push off my covers and crawl to the end of the bed where my clothes are. I dress fast and run down to the kitchen.

Cass is sitting at the table, chewing her tiny fingernails.

Eat your cereal before it gets soggy, she says. Cass is skinny-skinny and her face is bony and sharp to look at.

Does Dad know? I ask her. She stops chewing on her fingernails and leans forward. Her face gets bigger. Her eyebrows go up and her eyes look like heavy, black stones.

About what? she asks.

School, I say.

She shakes her head.

I look down at the table to think.

Come on, says Cass.

At the end of the driveway, the green car is lonely and wet with dew. I have to squint because the sun is making the car sparkly bright. Across the bumper, Cass put stickers that say, CLINTON GORE in red, white, and blue.

Is it winter? I ask Cass.

Not yet, she says.

The car smells cold inside.

Seat belt, Cass says.

The buckle is so cold I can't really even feel it when I put it on. I sit back and wait for the seat to get warmer. Cass starts the car and flicks on the wipers to clean the dew off the windshield. Then we go.

Cass is happy in the car. She pushes the eject button on the tape player and her tape flies out into the backseat. We laugh. The green car is so old we've had it since before I was born. It used to be Mother's and then Mother gave it to Cass. Now Cass has to share it with Leo because he learned how to drive, too.

I look out my window and watch the houses go by. There are also big, green parks and grocery stores with empty parking lots and there's the new bank and the movie theater made out of bricks with a sign that says, THE MIGHTY DUCKS in red letters that glow at night. We go faster now past houses and more houses. They are tall and close together. I watch how the colors change from light brown to yellow to dark brown to light blue. If I turn my head and look straight at the houses going by, I can make the colors blur into tan.

Cass rolls down her window a little.

Put yours down, she says.

I do it and the cold wind from outside blows through. Cass's long yellow hair flies and snaps around her face in the wind. She puts on her black stocking cap. Then she reaches back and hands me a scarf from the backseat. I bunch it up into a ball and hold it against my chest like a pillow.

You know, Cass says, you're going to be okay. The car is windy inside, so Cass has to make her voice louder than the wind.

Sebby, she says.

I look at her. She's facing straight ahead and talking to the road.

I'm sorry about yesterday in the library, Cass says. I'm sorry I said that you looked dead.

The word starts going in my head. I know the word *dead*. I hear it over and over again. I have to catch it and then my head is quiet.

I make up a song:

Dead, dead, dead
Sorry, Mother
Sorry, Mother, that you are dead
Don't be sad
Don't be sad that you are dead.

I sing the song to myself.

Cass puts her hand on my leg. In my head, the song won't stop. I close my eyes.

You'll be okay, Cass tells me.

Mother got married on a sunny day. She married Dad outside in the grass and the grass kept making her sneeze. Her eyes were watery and sad, but it was because of her allergies, she said. Cass was already there, inside of her stomach. Mother could feel the baby kicking inside her the whole time. The baby kicked until Mother kissed Dad and then the baby stopped kicking.

Where was I? I asked Mother.

You were up there in the trees, Mother said.

Now I remember sitting up high in the trees. I was happy and I kept jumping from one tree to another and the branches scraped my arms and legs when I jumped and landed, and jumped and landed. I had scratches all over. I could see the red scratches, but I couldn't feel them because I wasn't really me yet. I was just a part of Mother floating up in the trees.

Hello, Cass says, earth to Sebby?

I can't answer. She pulls the car over to the side of the road and we stop. Everything stops, but in my head the song about Mother keeps going. *Don't be sad that you are dead.* Cass puts her cold hand on my cheek and turns my face to look at her. She holds still and I hold still. Then Cass smiles because she's going to tickle me. I know she's going to tickle me. I count in my head. One, two, three. I'm ready. But then Cass jumps in her seat and I scream. She tickles under my arms and all over. I laugh until I run out of air. Cass is laughing, too. I'm kicking and trying to wiggle loose, but Cass holds on tight.

Okay, okay, she says and she stops. You're a good boy, she tells me.

I move back over to my seat. I'm tired. The inside of my mouth is dry like I just woke up.

Cass gets out of the car to smoke a cigarette. She leans against the door, so all I can see is her back and the smoke twisting up. Cass says that she smokes because it gives her time to think.

Straight ahead, the empty white sky gets brighter. I look down at my lap, but the white sky glow stays and makes me see glowing spots all over. It's true that the sun can make you blind if you look at it for too long. I close my eyes tight and think about how the sun fills up the whole sky with light. Then my head is quiet and there's the sound of trees growing, stretching up and up. The trees are growing and making everything else small.

Cass opens the door and gets back in.

Sebby? she asks. Are you sleeping?

I don't say anything. Cass smells like smoke.

You're a good boy, she says again.

Cass drives and we blow past the trees. They say, Shhhhhh.

I let the trees put me to sleep.

Grandmother Bernie locked the windows shut and in the summer, her air conditioner kept breaking, so the air in her house got heavy and dirty-tasting. It made Mother dizzy. She fell asleep on the couch and Dad had to clap his hands on her cheeks to wake her up. After that, Dad put in a ceiling fan.

I lay on my back under the fan. I could make my eyes follow just one blade around and around and then the fan looked like it was slowing down. But Grandmother Bernie wanted me to sit on her lap always. She held me close like a baby and hummed with the fan. You couldn't hear the fan unless you listened for it. Grandmother Bernie hummed and held me close, so I could hear her voice humming inside her chest. It sounded like a motor deep down in the ocean.

Let him go play, Mother would say, he's not a baby anymore.

When we stayed the night, Grandmother Bernie made me sleep in the crib with the cold, plastic mattress that crinkled.

The crib was in Grandmother Bernie's room next to her closet. She left the closet light on for a nightlight. I could count all her shoes, stacked up high in clear plastic shoe boxes with ugly, green-colored lids. Cass and I would sneak into her room during the day and Cass read me the names of all the shoe boxes, so I knew them in my head. Beige Heel, Black Aerosoles, Pink/Orange Flat, Brown Suede Tassel.

Grandmother Bernie said good night and fell asleep just like that. Her snores came out like whistles.

She asked me once why I crawled out the window. Mother was helping her make a broccoli casserole that smelled like cheese, and I was sitting on the counter watching.

I don't remember why, I said.

Mother's face got red and angry.

It was an accident, Mother said. Her eyes were watery and she turned away.

Louise, Grandmother Bernie said. She put her hand on Mother's back.

I wake up a little bit. We're still in the car, driving. Cass's window is open and the car feels windy, cold and empty. I want her to pull over so the wind and cold and everything will stop. I have to pee so bad it hurts. I don't think I can hold it.

Cass, I say. My voice sounds scratchy and asleep. I can feel my throat getting tight and then I'm crying.

Sebby, Cass says, what is it? She pulls the car over to the side of the road.

I unlock my door and run out. I have to jump over the rail where the road stops and then I run and slide down the gravel and dirt into the trees. I can't get my zipper down. I'm crying and it's hard to see. My fingers are still asleep. I shake out my hands and try the zipper again and then it works. My pee comes out fast and quiet. Cass keeps calling my name. I can hear her coming, looking for me. I don't say anything. I watch how the dirt soaks up my pee.

Cass grabs my shoulders and shakes me hard.

What's wrong? Cass asks.

I tell her I had to pee. I thought I was going to have an accident and I couldn't say the words. There wasn't enough time to say the words. My face is wet and cold. I can feel my nose running and it tickles above my lip.

Did you have a bad dream? Cass asks me. She wipes my face with the red scarf and takes my hand. I let her pull me back to the car.

Cass drives and it's quiet except I can't stop sniffling.

Where are we going? I ask her.

To visit Emma, Cass says.

Emma quit school and moved far away to grow bees and make honey at a farm. Now she has a baby girl.

I don't want to see Emma.

When I'm old enough to drive the green car, I will go all the way to Disney World in Florida. Mother took us for a vacation once and she bought me a puzzle of how the states fit together so I could see where we were driving. There is also a Disneyland in California, but that is so far away. And now there's a Euro Disney in Paris that opened on April 12. You can't drive there. You have to fly in an airplane. Leo saved the Disney World map of where all the rides are and he circled the best ones in yellow. It's in his desk drawer.

I'm hungry, I tell Cass.

Okay, she says, we'll be there soon. Cass reaches over to get a tape out of the glove compartment. The tape is black with a white label that says, THE CLASH LONDON CALLING FOR CASS XOXO A. The letters are tall and skinny and red. Cass pushes in the tape. Her mouth moves and makes all the words to the song, but her voice doesn't come out or maybe she's just whispering the words. I don't know who A is.

A is for Alexander, like Uncle Alexander. He was Mother's brother and then he died of cancer. I remember Uncle Alexander playing tennis in white shorts and socks pulled all the way up.

I was in the guest bedroom looking at the shells in their glass case. I like to take the shells out and then put them back in a different way, sometimes from smallest to biggest or sometimes from lightest to darkest.

I couldn't find you, Mother said. Uncle Alexander is dead, she whispered.

I kept taking the shells out. I thought about Uncle Alexander playing tennis.

Mother told him, You look ridiculous when you run, it's like you're dancing.

In my head, I tried to see Uncle Alexander in regular clothes, but I couldn't. I took out the littlest shell and stared at it.

Well, Mother said and looked up.

I looked up, too.

I'm lost, she said to the ceiling.

Then I looked at her face. I didn't understand.

Can you see that? she asked and pointed up. A bird, she said.

I could see it, too, in the white-frosting paint. The shape like a bird with its wings spread out.

Mother left me with the shells. I put them back in the case from quietest to loudest and that was almost the same as smallest to biggest.

We're close, Cass says, maybe ten more minutes.

In front of us, the sun is low. Cass squints to see the road. We're driving next to the ocean. It's dark, dark blue. The ocean's like a night with no moon.

Are we still in Massachusetts? I ask her.

No, she says, this is New Hampshire.

Have I ever been in New Hampshire before? I ask her.

Maybe, she says.

I know where New Hampshire is on my puzzle map of the United States and how the shape of it is kind of like a triangle. New Hampshire is a light blue puzzle piece and Massachusetts is purple. I try to think about whether it feels different to be here, in a different color and a different shape. I don't think so.

We make a turn and then the road gets bumpy.

It's somewhere close, Cass says.

I look around for a house.

Oh, there, Cass says. She points.

The house where Emma lives is white with a red door and red paint around the windows. There's Emma on the front steps and a baby on a pink blanket in the grass. The baby keeps standing up, then falling. Emma waves to us. Her hair is short like boy hair, because she shaved her head to be the same as Sinéad O'Connor, who sings the song on the radio "Nothing Compares 2 U." That song makes me think of Mother, how many days and weeks and months she's been gone. I used to always know, but now I try to figure it out. It's more than five months.

Cass parks in the long driveway and gets out of the car quickly. She runs to Emma.

The baby's gotten so big, Cass says, and her voice comes out loud and shaky because she's running.

Emma stands up to hug Cass.

I stay by the car. I want to get back in and go to sleep.

Hello, Sebastian, Emma says.

I wave.

Come on, says Cass.

I start walking toward them. Emma picks up her baby and the blanket and we go up the front steps.

Bees, the baby says to the black-and-white picture of a beehive on the wall.

We have to take off our shoes and put them on the shoe rack.

House rules, Emma says.

I pull off my socks, too, because they're wet from my feet sweating. The floor is cold wood. I walk on my tiptoes.

In the kitchen, we sit on yellow chairs. There are maps on the walls with dark arrows and lines drawn on them. I don't understand the arrows and the fat, black lines, but I think they mean something bad.

I'll make tea, Emma says. You have to taste our honey.

Is nobody home? Cass asks.

They're on vacation, says Emma. They left me to watch over everything. Can you hold her? she asks.

The baby wiggles and kicks on Cass's lap.

Oh, what's the matter? Cass asks her in a small voice and then makes a shushing noise.

The baby's face looks ready to cry. Cass bounces her up and down.

There you go, Cass whispers close to the baby's ear.

You guys hungry? Emma asks. I can make something quick.

Emma's taking things out of the refrigerator and Cass is bouncing the baby. They're not looking, so I slide off my chair and sit down under the table. There are six rolled-up posters leaning against the wall in the corner. I reach out and grab one. Then I unroll it slowly so the paper stays quiet and doesn't crinkle. I have to hold one end down with my feet and one end down with my hands. The poster is another map with fat, black arrows that move from the bottom to the top.

Those are the directed paths of the killer bees, Emma says.

I turn and she's squatting right there behind me.

Oh, I say. I move off the map and watch how it rolls back up.

Sebby, get up here, Cass says.

I crawl out and sit back down in the same yellow chair.

He hides under tables now, Cass says to Emma.

But I wasn't even hiding.

Peanut butter and honey, Emma says and she hands me a plate of sandwiches cut into triangles. This is fall honey so it's a little bit spicy, she says, spring honey is sweeter.

I take a bite and I'm glad because it's not spicy to me.

How's school? she asks me.

Teacher's name is Ms. Lambert, I tell her.

Oh, Emma says and smiles at me.

So what do you think of your beloved Sinéad O'Connor? Cass asks.

I know what Sinéad O'Connor did. She ripped up a picture of the pope's face. The pope has a happy, old face with red cheeks.

I'm growing my hair out, Emma says. It's totally stupid. She doesn't even know what she means. She just likes to stir shit up.

Totally, Cass says. She shakes her head and then she says, So I ran into Mickey the other day at Tower Records.

Cass and Emma laugh then.

How's the rest of the class of '92? Emma asks.

We're fucking fantastic, says Cass. She's trying not to laugh. How're you?

Proud to be a nongraduate, Emma says.

Cass and Emma laugh some more. Then they stop and it's quiet for a little bit. Cass sits up straighter and folds her hands together. She doesn't eat any of the sandwiches.

How's your Dad? Emma asks.

He's skinny, Cass says, and he has a beard now.

You know, Emma says, maybe you need to get away for a while. You could stay here as long as you want.

We'll see, Cass says. You know what's funny? she asks. Guess what song was playing when my parents met?

What? Emma asks.

"Satisfaction," Cass says and she laughs.

I know what happened. At the place called Sandy's Escape, Dad asked Mother to dance.

Mother said, Okay, if you'll hold my cigarettes.

Dad put them in the chest pocket of his shirt and then they danced. I think the cigarettes were there to protect Dad's heart. His heart is what fell in love with Mother.

Can I go look at the maps? I ask Emma. I point under the table.

Sure, she tells me.

I lie down on my stomach and close my eyes. I listen to the quiet of the floor and the ground underneath until the quiet starts to hum. Then Cass's voice goes away.

I remember at the birthday party Katya took me to the paddle-boats on the lake.

You is very scared? Katya asked me.

The boat rocked when I got in so I sat down fast and held on. Katya stood up to show me she was not very scared. You can see how tall Katya is when she stands up. She's tall because she's a year older than everyone else in third grade. She came from Russia last December. Teacher says it's our job to help her learn English. I'm a good helper. The other kids teach Katya to say things like buttface or shitcakes or I'm-too-sexy-for-my-shirt, but I don't do that.

Katya splashed water on me.

Stop, I told her, please, Katya.

I'm scared of lakes.

Katya stopped. Katya is nice because she has nice eyes. They're brownish yellow. I didn't know eyes could have yellow in them, but now I know. Katya has perfect hands, too. They're clean. In class, Katya keeps getting up to wash her hands and Teacher has to tell her to sit down. I like to watch Katya's clean hands open the tin of candies she hides inside her desk. Katya is good at eating candy because she never bites into the pieces. She can suck on the candy until it looks like just a tiny crystal on her tongue. She opens her mouth and shows me.

Katya steered the boat all the way down where we couldn't see the birthday party anymore. I wanted to turn around.

Katya, I said.

She was not hearing me. We kept going all the way down to the wooden bridge and then we got stuck in the mud. I wanted to crawl out of the boat and climb up the mud to the bridge.

Katya grabbed my arm and said, No.

My heart beat louder and louder. In my ears I could hear my heart. Katya laughed and shook her head at me. I looked around. There was nobody to see us. I rocked back and forth to make the boat come loose, but nothing happened. Katya put her hands on my shoulders to make me be still, and there was so much time. It made me sick to my stomach how I could feel so much time, years and years. Katya put her face close. She put her mouth on my mouth and kissed.

I fell backward and hit my head. I could see the sky and a bird. The bird was so high up that it looked like a frozen still, black dot. I blinked. The sun was white-hot and everything in my head got brighter like my head was filling up with light.

The floor is cold and hard now. I pull myself up onto the yellow chair.

Cass's voice is saying, I'm just not going to worry about it. She looks at me and says, I don't know why you're so tired.

I don't say anything. I put my chin down on the table.

Emma gets a book about bees from the bookshelf.

See, Emma says, they're kind of fuzzy and cute.

Cass nods at the picture.

Some breeders are using the killer bees now, Emma says. They kill the queens and take over.

You have killer bees? Cass asks.

Emma shakes her head, no. The baby points at the picture of the killer bee and giggles. She's sitting in her high chair. When she giggles, juice spills out of her mouth and onto her shirt. She kicks her puffy red feet up in the air. Emma reaches over and squeezes the baby's foot.

Can I call Dad? I ask Cass.

She pushes up her sleeve to look at her watch and then she turns to Emma.

Can we use the phone? she asks.

Sure, Emma says, it's in there. She points to the room across the hall.

You can go call, Cass says to me. Tell him we're spending the night.

I push back my chair and it scrapes on the floor.

Careful, Sebby, Cass says.

In the other room, there's a black leather couch that smells new and a wooden table with an old-fashioned phone. Through two big glass doors, you can see outside to a patio with tall yellow flowers. I sit down on the couch and pick up the phone. I like it better in here because there's carpet to rub my feet on. Cass yells at me from the kitchen. She says that from here you have to dial 1-6-1-7 first.

I dial our whole phone number.

We're at Emma's house, I tell Dad.

Jesus Christ, he says.

I'm staring at the painting on the wall. It's of this white house and the farm all around it. The house looks small in the picture and the outside looks so big.

Sebby, are you there? Dad asks.

Uh-huh, I say. Cass says we're spending the night.

Are you all right? Dad asks me.

I guess so, I say. I feel my eyes getting hot and watery. I close my eyes hard to make the tears go back inside. I'm moving my feet fast, back and forth on the carpet.

Can you put Cass on the phone? he asks.

Cass, I call for her.

She comes and grabs the phone out of my hand. Emma comes, too.

We have lots of movies, Emma says. You want to watch one?

I don't know, I say. My eyes are hurting. I rub them hard until I can see bright colors and shapes flashing.

Sebby, Emma says. I open my eyes and it takes a second before the black goes away and I can see again.

I'll show you what we've got, she says.

Emma opens one of the wooden cabinets and inside is a big TV.

Here, she says. She pulls open a drawer full of movies.

I pick out *The Sound of Music* and hand it to her.

Okay, says Emma.

I watch how she puts in the tape and pushes PLAY. It works the same way as our VCR at home.

I like how the movie starts with the lady, Maria, singing, even though she's all by herself. Sometimes I like to pretend a camera is watching me when I'm alone. I do things like stick out my tongue or say the words I'm thinking. The camera watches and listens.

Do you want to sit? Emma asks me. She points to the couch behind me.

Fine, Cass says and she hangs up the phone.

Everything okay? asks Emma.

Cass nods and points to the TV. Sebby's in love with Julie Andrews, she tells Emma. He doesn't believe me when I tell him that she's a grandma now.

Emma laughs.

We've seen this movie, like, a million times, Cass says, forward and back.

At the end, I used to have to watch the whole thing in slow rewind to the beginning. Maria and the children moved backward and undid all their singing and dancing. Then the movie was new again.

Cass keeps talking and it's hard to hear the TV, so I stand closer. I don't like this part in the church with the nuns who have big heads. I go up to the VCR and push the arrow button to fast-forward.

Emma's baby laughs at nothing. She's sitting down on the floor with her soft blocks.

We're going out back to see the bees, Cass says. You'll be okay in here.

The movie is at the part where the captain calls the kids with his whistle and then they all line up in a row. The kids look so nice together in their matching clothes. I think about how if I could be in the Von Trapp family I'd stand in Brigitta's place, between Marta and Kurt.

Howareyou, I think the baby says to the TV.

What? I ask, but she ignores me.

She puts a block in her mouth and chews on it.

You're weird, I tell her.

She looks at me and the block falls out of her mouth. I watch her crawl over to the glass doors and then I follow. She puts her hand on the glass.

Outside, a tiny black bird lands on the deck and holds still like a statue. I knock on the glass door to make it fly away. The bird flaps its wings and looks at me sideways with one eye. We stare at each other.

It's okay, I say to the baby. I grab her under the arms and

pull her back, away from the bird. Then I pick her up. She's warm and heavy. I hold her tight and take big, slow steps down the hall to the back of the house. I have to find the door to the backyard. The baby wiggles and I tell her to stop.

I hold her with just one arm so I can pull open the screen door and then turn the doorknob. I do it fast and the baby slips down my side a little bit. The screen door bangs shut behind us.

There's a path that goes straight out and then down a hill. I can't see where it ends.

Cass! I yell. I hold still and wait for her to answer, but it's quiet. In the sky, the moon is thin like a tiny cloud and not glowing yet. Soon, it will be night.

I try to walk, but the path is gravelly and I don't have my shoes and socks on. Tiny rocks stick in my feet and hurt. I have to go slow. The baby wiggles and kicks and starts to cry. She's too heavy. I sit down with her on the dusty path. Her crying is so loud.

You be quiet, I tell her. I try to pick the pieces of gravel out of my heels and then I'm crying, too. I think it's the baby's fault.

She keeps crying loud. The wind blows the dust up all around us and it sticks to her wet, red cheeks. I feel bad for her.

I'm sorry, I say and I hold her hand.

Sebastian! Cass's voice shouts. She looks like a tiny X all the way down the path. Cass and Emma run to us.

Are you okay? Cass asks me.

I nod. Cass is breathing hard. Her hair is all messy from the wind. She picks me up. Emma is holding the baby and wiping her dirty face.

What happened? Cass asks. Her voice is fast and scared.

I tell her there was a mean bird staring at me and the baby. I thought something bad was going to happen.

A bird! Emma yells. Did you try to carry her out here?

Emma's looking at me. I don't say anything. I put my head on Cass's shoulder.

He didn't know, Cass says. He thought he was doing the right thing.

I used to wake up in the middle of the night and wait for Mother to come and put me in my old stroller. I used to wake up and sometimes I heard her go without me.

I wasn't with her when she got hit by the car. There was a baby in her stomach and the baby died, too.

Now I wake up in the quiet and the first thing I know is that Mother's not here. I wake up and it scares me. Mother's dead, I tell myself.

I'm wearing clothes from yesterday. Next to me in the bed, Cass is breathing long, slow breaths. The room is gray-dark and shadowy.

Cass, I say, but not loud enough to wake her up. I poke her shoulder and she doesn't move.

Cass, I whisper. I try poking her shoulder harder, but nothing happens.

I close my eyes. I know what to do. I just have to keep my eyes closed until I fall back to sleep again. I take long, slow breaths like Cass.

The next time I wake up, the room is sunny. Cass will wake up soon and we'll go. I'm not scared now. I just have to wait. There's a tree shadow on the wall. I watch how the shadow branches move in the wind.

I think of the "Bobby McGee" song and I can hear it in my head. The best part is the *La da da da da* part. It sounds kind of happy and sad and I know she's thinking about secret things she can't say, because I asked Mother and that's what she told me. "Bobby McGee" used to be my favorite song with Cass. In the backseat of the green car, we listened to it on my orange and blue Fisher-Price tape player. I pushed REWIND and played it again and again. Cass sang all the words with me. We were driving to see Grandmother Bernie, because she was lonely in her big house. Mother and Dad were sitting in the front seat, listening to talking on the radio. Leo was leaning forward, trying to hear the news.

Sebby, Cass says. She rolls onto her back. Hi, she says.

Hi, I tell her.

Cass is quiet and still again. Then she sits up. Her clothes are wrinkly.

Is it time to go? I ask her.

Soon, she says.

Cass walks over to the big egg-shaped mirror by the door. She stands close and stares at her sleepy face. She touches the sharp bones under her cheeks and then moves her hand away. Her eyes look too big and the freckles on the tops of her cheeks are darker in the mirror.

I'll say bye to Emma, Cass says. You get ready to go.

I sit on the end of the bed and swing my legs. I watch them and it's like they're moving all by themselves. In my head I count because counting is better than waiting.

Okay, Cass says, let's go. She's standing in the hallway.

I stop my legs and slide down off the bed. At the front door, we sit down to put on our shoes. Mine feel hard and stiff from getting so cold.

I follow Cass out to the car.

Why do you always have to walk behind me? she asks.

I don't really know why. I take fast steps and try to walk next to her.

Dad's waiting for us in the kitchen. He's sitting with his elbows on the table. Between his elbows, there's his black coffee mug with steam twisting up. I walk over to him. Dad grabs me and holds me against his loud chest. I put my hand over his heart and feel it beating. Dad stands up with me. He walks in circles around the table.

Goddamn it, he says. He sets me down and looks at me with his hands on my shoulders and then he hugs me too hard.

Mother used to put her hand on my forehead and say, My son, you're going to live for a very long time—I can feel all of the life inside of you.

I closed my eyes and I could feel it, too. I could feel my chest getting warmer and warmer and that was the life inside of me.

In the morning, Dad asks me if I want to go to school. I can stay home with him since he's not going to his office today. In his office, Dad's writing a book about music.

Okay, I say, I'll stay.

Dad's hair is messy. He's wearing his pajamas, a green T-shirt that says KISS ME I'M IRISH, and gray sweatpants.

Hop on, Dad says. He gives me a piggyback ride down to the kitchen.

I sit at the table and watch him make eggs.

Your teacher called, he tells me. Dad doesn't turn around. He keeps cooking the eggs.

I stare at his back.

Do you have a note for me? he asks.

I tore it up, I say. I say the words fast to make them go away.

Dad still doesn't turn around.

Well, he says, I made you an eye appointment this afternoon because your teacher thinks you might need glasses.

Dad turns off the stove, but the eggs keep sizzling. He tips them out of the pan and onto my plate. Now the eggs are quiet.

I need a haircut, I say.

Dad rubs his face with his big hands and sits down at the table with me.

You want Denise to cut your hair? Dad asks.

I look at him. He takes a sip of his coffee.

Yes, I say. Denise always cuts my hair. Can we go right now? I ask.

Whenever you're ready, Dad says.

I don't want to eat my eggs, so I run upstairs. Cass's door is still closed. I want to knock and make her wake up, but if I do, then she'll stop being nice, so I run past her door and down the hall to my room. I can lay out clean clothes by myself. I pick out jeans and my light blue sweatshirt that has the mean grizzly bear on the back. I set clean underwear and socks on top of the pile. Then I'm ready to get dressed.

My jeans feel cold when I pull them on. I have to rub my legs to make them warmer. I hear Cass's door open. She walks by and then comes back.

What're you doing? Cass asks. She holds on to the wall and leans into my room.

Nothing, I say. I'm not going to school, I tell her, and I feel happy to say it. I run past Cass, down the stairs, to Dad.

Dad's lying facedown on the floor. His music is turned down low. I sit on Dad's back like he's a flat horse.

What's this music called? I ask him.

Vivaldi, Dad says. He pushes himself up on his hands and knees.

I hold on to his shoulders and he tries to buck me off. I let go and fall. Dad tickles me on the floor.

You ready? he asks.

I nod.

Run upstairs and get my sneakers, says Dad.

I go as fast as I can.

I open the closet that was Dad and Mother's together. I know there's a secret door at the very back that goes into a low room called a crawl space, because Mother showed it to me. I reach my hand in, past all the clothes, and touch the doorknob. It feels cold.

Dad's sneakers are lined up on his side. Mother's shoes are all packed up in brown boxes. I put my hand on the box that I know has Mother's red slippers with the sequins. The red slippers were Mother's favorite shoes to wear even though they were just slippers and not really shoes. Mother said if she went to a ball she would wear her red slippers. I want to hide the box in my closet so it will be mine and no one else will touch it.

I go into the hall and look. Cass is not there. I walk with the box behind my back. I walk slow and quiet to my room, but then Cass is standing there, looking out my window.

Oh, I say.

Cass turns around.

What do you have? she asks me.

Nothing, I say.

I back out of my room with the box behind my back.

Sebby! Cass yells at me.

I hold the box tight against my chest and run back to Mother's room.

Cass runs after me.

Those aren't yours, Cass says. Leave her stuff alone.

I put Mother's shoes back in the closet. Then I grab Dad's sneakers. I push past Cass and run downstairs.

Did you hear me? Cass shouts.

Five steps from the bottom, I jump. I land and then fall forward on my knees, but I don't drop Dad's sneakers. I get up and run to him.

Here, I say. I'm out of breath.

Thanks, Dad says.

Cass comes downstairs then.

You get mad at me for taking him out of school and then you do the same thing, says Cass. No wonder he thinks it's optional. Her voice is loud.

Dad's putting on his sneakers. Let's talk about this later, he says.

Cass turns and goes to the kitchen. Right, she says, later.

I'm watching Dad's face.

Don't worry about it, he says to me.

We go out to the car. I reach up and hold Dad's hand. He's still wearing his T-shirt and sweatpants.

Look, Dad says. He points at our tall tree in the front yard.

It's losing leaves and the ones that are still on it are reddish orange, colors like fire.

The bell on the door jingles when Dad and I go in. Denise is sweeping brown hair into a pile on the floor. She stops to look at us.

I haven't seen you in forever, she says.

Denise's shop is called Guys and Dolls. A long time ago, she used to put makeup on actors in Chicago and fix their hair. She likes to make a small pinch in the air with her fingers and say, Look, honey, do you see this?—this is how close I was to marrying Sky Masterson.

Good to see you, says Dad. Denise looks back down at the floor and sweeps again.

I can see her face turning sad and I know that she's remembering about Mother.

Stephen, she says to Dad in a softer voice, how are you?

I need a haircut, I say.

Denise comes over and puts her hand on my head. She combs my hair with her fingers. It feels nice how she does that.

Such beautiful hair, she says, it gets wasted on a boy. She puts her hands on my shoulders and pushes me over to one of the special chairs.

I'll take care of him, she says to Dad.

Okay, Dad says, I'll just sit and read. He points to the pile of magazines.

Dad is shy because of what Denise did at one of Mother's Christmas parties. Dad doesn't like parties, so he drinks wine and then falls asleep sitting in a chair. Mother and Denise put pink curlers in Dad's hair when he was sleeping. He woke up and drank more wine and then he let them finish. Mother told that story over and over again.

Denise pumps the back of my chair and I go up. She wraps a silky smock around me and Velcros it behind my neck. I have to be still now. In the mirror, my face looks whiter and my eyes look darker.

Denise sprays my hair with a water bottle. I close my eyes and listen to the scissors cutting. Denise knows I like the sound of the scissors so she doesn't talk to me or ask me any questions.

When she's done, she takes off the smock and brushes the back of my neck with a brush that's like a fat paintbrush to get off all the loose hairs.

She lowers me down and I go to look in the bowl of prizes. There are lollipops, fuzzy stickers, and plastic rings. I look for an orange lollipop.

Thank you, I hear Dad say.

No problem, Denise says.

You should bring him in every two months or so, she tells him.

I find my lollipop and turn around to look at them.

How much do I owe you? asks Dad.

Denise waves her hand and shakes her head.

No, really, Dad says.

Denise smiles. She looks very different from Mother. You can see she has big boobs under her blue sweater. I don't know if Dad likes how Denise looks. Dad won't really look at her. He keeps looking out the window.

I'm going out for my coffee break, Denise says. I'll walk you to your car.

She puts up a sign in the front window that says BACK SOON and locks the door behind us. Next to Denise's shop is the Laundromat that has a gumball machine and the Chinese restaurant, Don't Wok on By.

I think how if people see us together, they might think Denise is my Mom. I don't like that. I want to run, but Dad grabs my hand. I walk faster, and try to pull him with me. Dad squeezes my hand harder.

Stop, he whispers. We're all the way over there, Dad says and points to our car in the middle of the parking lot. Cass put a CLINTON GORE sticker on Dad's bumper, too. He doesn't care.

I'm headed this way, Denise says and nods at the Dunkin' Donuts.

Well, thank you, says Dad.

Denise smiles again. Then she waves and walks the other way.

Say thank you, Dad whispers to me.

Thank you! I yell out to her.

The doctor asks me if I've been having any trouble with my eyes.

I shrug. Dad should've come in here with me to answer her questions.

The doctor keeps smiling and she talks really slowly. She has a stretchy mouth. I don't like her face.

Okay, she says, first I'm going to look at the outside of your eyes and make sure they look healthy. She shines a light on me.

I blink hard. I want to rub my eyes, but I can't do that in front of her.

How old are you now, Sebastian? she asks me.

Eight, I tell her.

She smiles too big. Okay, she says, I'm going to ask you to look at some letters. She walks across the room and pulls down a chart.

Go ahead and read me the smallest row of letters you can see, she tells me.

I squint at the chart. My eyes hurt. I feel hot in my cheeks and under my arms.

Just do your best, the doctor says.

I try. Then the doctor gives me lenses to look through and I keep trying to read the small letters.

Okay, Sebastian, the doctor says, I'm going to go out and get your dad. She leaves me alone in the room.

I look around. Hanging on the wall, there's a pair of giant

metal glasses. In one lens is a big, round clock. In the other, it says, Time to get your eyes checked!

When the doctor comes back with Dad, she says, Sebastian, you are going to need glasses. Then she looks at Dad and says, I think Sebastian's eye muscles may have tightened. It can happen when vision goes uncorrected for too long and the eyes try to overcompensate. His last visit was, let me see. She looks at her notes and then says, Over a year ago. We won't know his exact prescription until the muscles relax.

Dad looks down at his lap. His hands are folded neatly.

The doctor tells me to go out to the waiting room. She needs to talk to Dad alone.

There are Legos out there, she says, and books.

I stand up and look at Dad. He nods. My chest feels tight and it's hard to breathe. I can only take little breaths.

I find things with my new glasses.

On the sidewalk at the end of our driveway, there's a dead butterfly getting eaten by ants. I lie down on my stomach to watch. My eyes still hurt, but I can see more now. I can see all the tiny ant legs walking over the butterfly.

Leo comes with his big, red backpack on.

What're you doing? he asks. He stands there and waits for me.

I can see his feet standing, waiting, but I don't get up, so he leaves.

I watch the ants. There are more and more, covering the butterfly and turning it black.

The sky's getting dark and the ants are harder to see. I have to squint at them. I feel cold, but I'm stuck. I need to watch until the butterfly is gone.

Dad comes out to get me. I let him pick me up. He carries me inside like a baby. My face is cold. I reach up and put my hand on Dad's cheek. I hold my hand there.

Dad carries me upstairs and takes off my glasses and my shoes. He tucks me into bed with my clothes on.

Before Mother married Dad, she was a girl who lived in a white house. She had a cat named Duncan and he was the same color white as the house. On the day Duncan died under the bushes in the backyard, Mother found his body and she ran.

She was running and running to get the cat out of her head. She kept running to make him not dead and then she fell.

I remember like I was floating there, watching.

The lady with shiny gray hair helped Mother up. Mother's hands were stinging and her knees were bloody and hot.

Oh dear, the lady said.

Mother was not crying. She was looking at her red, scraped hands and thinking of the cat.

Let's clean you up, the lady said.

Mother followed her into a house. I remember Mother walked with her hands in front of her, palms turned up like she was showing them to the gray sky.

In a blue bathroom, the lady picked up Mother and sat her next to the sink.

What's your name, sweetheart? the lady asked.

Louise, Mother told her.

Such a grown-up name, the lady said.

On the wall, there were two blue fish with gold bubbles floating up out of their mouths. The lady cleaned Mother's hands and knees with a clear bottle of alcohol that she poured on cotton balls. The alcohol burned, but Mother didn't cry.

I pretend to be asleep still when Cass comes in to wake me up for school. She sits on the edge of my bed.

Sebby, she says, it's late.

I don't open my eyes.

I know you can hear me, Cass says and she stands up now.

Her slippers swish-walk away on the carpet. Then I wet the bed on purpose. I didn't think I would really do it, but then I do and I feel bad.

Cass, I say, I had an accident.

She walks over to me and lifts my blanket to see.

Are you kidding me? she asks. We don't have time for this.

I'm sorry, I say.

Cass grabs my shoulders and pulls me out of the bed.

Go take a shower, she says. This is so gross.

I watch Cass peel the wet sheet off my bed. She turns around and sees me watching.

Go, she says.

I run into the bathroom and turn on the shower. Then I take off my T-shirt. My wet pajama bottoms are stuck to my legs. I pull them down and get in the shower. I stand there under the hot water with my eyes closed. I am really sorry. Now Cass will be mean and I don't want to go to school.

There's knocking.

Sebby, Dad's voice says, we're late already, let's go.

I don't move. Dad knocks again.

Sebby, he says, are you okay?

I open my eyes now. Dad knocks and then comes in. He turns off the water and wraps a towel around me.

Did you hear me? he asks.

I don't say anything.

You have to hurry, Dad says and carries me into my room. Get your clothes on.

I look at my bed. All the blankets are gone. There's a dark wet stain on the blue mattress.

At lunch, Ronny's telling how you can make yourself faint. Katya and I don't sit at his table, but we're listening to him.

You have to breathe in and out really fast for thirty seconds, Ronny says, and then you stand up against a wall and someone has to push hard against your chest.

Katya's eating her apple slices. She eats just the white part and leaves the red skin. I don't feel very hungry. I'm holding my sandwich but not taking any bites.

I was passed out for almost a minute, Ronny says. He closes his eyes and falls forward on the table, like he's fainting.

Stupid, Katya whispers to me. She spits out a piece of apple skin and wipes her mouth on the back of her hand.

Ronny sits up again and laughs. He looks around at everybody watching him.

My sandwich drops out of my hand.

You don't like it? Katya asks and picks it up for me.

I shake my head. I remember the air in Grandmother's house and how it made Mother faint. I don't want to be sad in front of everyone, but my eyes are filling up and that feels like burning. I close my eyes and try to push it back down. Then I'm crying.

Sebby, Katya says.

I'm crying without making any noise. Katya pulls my glasses off.

Sebby, she says, what do you want?

The other kids are quiet now. I know they see me.

Hey, Katya, Andy says, what's the matter with the crybaby?

A balled-up napkin hits my cheek and lands in my lap. Katya picks it up and throws it back at Ronny's table.

What? Katya asks me. Sebby, she says, what do you want? She keeps asking me.

I'm looking at her skinny, pretty shoulder. Her yellow sweater is too small. The sleeves are short and tight. I lean forward and bite her shoulder as hard as I can. Katya doesn't move. Her yellow sweater tastes like soap.

Stop it, she says.

I stop and now Katya is crying, too.

The lunch-duty lady runs over to us.

What's going on here? she asks.

Ronny and one of the girls at his table tell her what I did.

I have to go home early from school. Dad's on his way to get me. I'm waiting for him in the principal's office.

Are you feeling okay? Dr. Fischer asks me again. He's sitting in a big, brown chair with his arms folded on the desk.

I look at him and nod.

When Dad comes, Dr. Fischer asks him to sit. In the chair next to mine, Dad stretches out his legs and crosses his ankles.

How're you? Dad asks.

Just fine, Dr. Fischer says. How are you and Sebastian doing?

Dad switches and crosses his ankles the other way. Then he looks up and says, I think we're all right.

Teaching's going well? Dr. Fischer asks.

Dad teaches at a college that's only for girls, but the teachers can be boys.

I'm on leave, Dad says, finishing my book.

Dr. Fischer nods and says, It might be best for Sebastian to stay home a few days.

Dad coughs and clears his throat.

Okay, Dad says, he may just need some extra rest.

I start to swing my feet. Without even looking, Dad reaches over and puts his hand on my knees to stop my feet.

I have to go to the bathroom, I say.

Hold on a minute, Dad says. He looks at Dr. Fischer and waits.

I'll give you a call on Friday, Dr. Fischer says, and we'll see how Sebastian's feeling then.

Friday's in two days, I say.

That's right, says Dr. Fischer. He looks down at the desk and moves some papers around. Very well, he says.

On Mother's funeral day, Leo helped me get dressed in a new suit that Cass bought for me. The light blue tie had tiny white stars all over it. Leo stood behind me in front of the mirror and tried to put the tie on me, but he couldn't do it right.

I have to get Dad, he said.

He left me in my room in front of the mirror. I was looking at my face and it was hard to breathe. I put my hand on the mirror to cover my face, because I didn't like how it looked.

Music started playing downstairs. The Otis Redding song about sitting on the dock.

Cass made Dad promise, no sad music. I think Otis Redding is sad music.

I went to Mother and Dad's room. Nobody was there and I wanted to go in the closet, so I did. Then I opened the secret door in the way back and crawled inside. The white stars all over my tie glowed in the dark.

I heard Leo calling for me and then Cass and Dad were calling for me, too. They couldn't find me, so Mrs. Franklin from next door had to come over and wait for me to come out. She walked all around the house calling my name, her voice getting louder and then quieter again. I knew that Dad and Cass and Leo went without me.

Leo wakes me up for dinner. It's almost six o'clock, he says. If you sleep anymore, you'll be up all night.

I'm sweaty from sleeping and my mattress is hot. I try reaching out with my foot to find a faraway spot that feels cool. Next to me, the wet stain from this morning is a smaller, dark blue egg.

Cass made you mashed potatoes, Leo says. He's leaning against the door with his arms folded.

I'm not hungry, I tell him.

Leo stands there, looking at me.

What? I ask him.

Nothing, Leo says. I wanted to tell you. Then he stops. He stands up straight and pushes his hands into his pockets.

I tried to throw a chair in fifth grade, Leo says. It was the day the spaceship launched. You know, the *Challenger*. We were watching and then it exploded on the TV. Mrs. Shapiro got up and, real calm, she turned off the TV and carried it out of the room. When she came back in, I remember she said, Sometimes these things happen. I hated her when she said that.

Leo stops again. I wait.

He says, Dad told me that the people on the spaceship were going to rescue Major Tom—the guy from the David Bowie song—and I kind of believed him. I started thinking about Major Tom floating around by himself in space with nobody to save him. Anyway, I picked up my chair and tried to throw it against the wall, but the chair was heavy and I couldn't really throw it so I sort of just dropped it and this girl, Angela, laughed at me. I had to go to the principal's office. I sat there crying.

Leo takes a step backward into the hallway.

Anyway, he says, it's time for dinner. Come on.

I used to write notes to Mother and hide them in places. I hid the notes in her books, in the pockets of her folded-up clothes, in her medicine drawer, in her pillowcase, in her shoes. If I wanted her to find the note fast, then I had to hide it in an easy place, like her purse.

I wrote her a note that said:

> To Mother,
>   Your name is Louise. Louise sounds like please. Louise please. Please Louise. Tell me what does Sebastian sound like?
>
>   From, Sebby

This note was not important, so I hid it in a hard place. I folded it up tiny and tight in her silver heart locket that has two small heart-shaped pictures. The pictures are of Uncle Alexander's face smiling and of Dad's face not smiling.

Mother brought me the notes when she found them. Sometimes she answered and sometimes she didn't.

It took her a very long time to find the note in her locket. I was in the backyard looking for snails. She sat down with me on the garden wall that's made out of rocks and she gave me back the note.

She said, You have a beautiful name. I can't think of any perfect rhymes, but it goes well with captain, she said, Captain Sebastian. Or stallion. Sebastian the stallion. Or action. Sebastian full of action.

BIRDS

On Friday, I go back to school. Cass drives me in the green car and drops me off in front.

Hey, she says, don't let all the little bastards get you down. She grabs my hand and squeezes it hard.

I have to run to my classroom to get there before the second bell rings.

At the front of the room, Teacher's sitting on her desk with her hands tucked under her legs. She smiles at me and nods. I know she still likes me even though I bit Katya.

Ms. Lambert. Lamb like a soft, white lamb and Bert, like on *Sesame Street*. It's a funny name to think about. In my head, I call her Teacher, but out loud I have to call her Ms. Lambert. My last name doesn't have two things put together like Teacher's name does. My last name is just Lane, like a lane you walk down or like a lane on the road for cars. It's nothing to think about.

Okay, Teacher says, who can tell me how many pounds of trash one person makes in a single day?

I fold my arms on my desk and rest my chin on my hands. The desk smells like scratchy blue cleaning powder.

Teacher looks around the room. Her lips are pressed together tight. I don't know the answer even though we've been learning about how to take care of the earth since the beginning of the year. I keep looking over at Katya, but she won't look at me.

Who remembers? Teacher asks.

Marianne raises her hand and answers. About four pounds, she says.

Teacher nods and tells her good job. Now, she asks, who can tell me a kind of material that is NOT biodegradable? She calls on Ryan.

Styrofoam, Ryan says.

Good, Teacher says. What else?

Some kinds of plastic and tinfoil, Frankie shouts.

Good, Teacher says, but please remember to raise your hand.

Stinky diapers! Ronny shouts without raising his hand and everybody starts laughing.

Teacher doesn't say anything and waits for quiet again. Her face turns red and she looks hard at Ronny. Her eyes don't move.

Today is your last day to finish your posters, she says.

We each have to make a poster about why recycling is important. Third-graders at all the schools have to make one, and whoever makes the best poster wins a new art set with paints and markers and colored pencils.

My poster is a picture of a regular trash can next to a re-cycling bin. In the trash can, all the bottles and cans are cry-ing, but in the recycling bin they're dancing and having a party. Teacher says I have to write something, too.

Like a catchy phrase, she says, that will stick in people's heads.

But I can't think of one.

Mica is the best drawer in our class and everybody knows she's going to win the new art set. She made a picture of what the world would look like without trees and animals. It's a lot of tall gray buildings and lonely, skinny people walking around with briefcases. Please recycle, she wrote across the top in her perfect block letters, I want a brighter future.

At morning recess, instead of meeting me under the tree, Katya plays jump rope with the girls. On her turn, all the girls sing, *Ice-cream soda, strawberry punch, tell me the name of your honeybunch. Is it A, B, C, D, E, F, G, H, I, J, K, L, M, N*—then Katya messes up and the girls scream out, Neill and Noah! Nathan Morris from Boyz II Men, someone says and then they all laugh. Katya laughs, too, and she covers her smile with both hands, like she really does love Neill or Noah or Nathan Morris.

I want to go home, so I run.

It's easy to run into the parking lot, down the hill, and out of school. Nobody chases me or yells at me to stop. I keep going fast down the street and I know I hate Katya and the whole stupid school.

The houses here are quiet and their colors are soft. They are light blue or light yellow or light green. One is light pink.

I see the grocery store at the end of the street. In the middle of the empty parking lot is a long line of shopping carts. I start walking now because I know where I can go. I can hide inside the grocery store.

The automatic doors slide open for me. I know where I'm going. There's room to hide where they keep all the vegetables and fruit. I find a space under the ledge that holds broccoli and lettuce. I duck underneath and sit hugging my legs against my chest. I'm okay here. I could stay for a long time, except it's cold. In front of me on the floor, I see a popcorn piece of Styrofoam. I reach out fast to grab it and put it in my pocket.

I wait for a long time. There's nothing to do, so sometimes I take the piece of Styrofoam out of my pocket to look at it.

I hear a cart coming down the aisle toward me. I wait and then it rolls past. I watch the feet go by. They're small feet. The shoes are very white and clean. I think the feet must be old lady feet because they go so slow. The old lady's shoes squeak on the grocery store floor and that sound makes me sad. I wait until the old lady is gone and then I crawl out from under the vegetables.

Outside, I find a pay phone. I push zero and then I dial Dad's number at work. The operator asks my name.

I hear my voice say, Sebby. Then the operator asks Dad if he'll take my call.

Yes, says Dad's voice. There's a clicking sound.

Sebby, Dad says, what're you doing?

Please come get me, I say. I close my eyes and pretend that I'm already gone. I'm flying through the dark line of space that connects my voice and Dad's voice. Space is a dark line that touches everywhere. Major Tom got lost because there's so much space.

Where are you? Dad's voice comes out louder now.

Sebby, he says even louder.

His voice scares me and I open my eyes. I tell him that I'm in front of the grocery store.

I'm coming, Dad says. Sit down, he tells me, don't move.

I sit on the cement in front of the pay phone and watch the empty gray parking lot. I watch until I see Dad's car coming.

At home, I go to the backyard and take the popcorn piece of Styrofoam out of my pocket. I dig a hole in the grass with a stick and put the Styrofoam in the hole. Then I cover it up with dirt.

I lie on my back and look up at the sky. I think about Katya. She's not my friend and I'm sorry. I keep looking up and then the sky starts to rain on me. I feel a cold drop on my forehead and also my cheek.

Sebby, Dad calls to me from the window, get in here.

I run inside, but I know the place in the grass where the Styrofoam is buried.

Dad watches me take off my shoes. His eyes are big and scared.

Go to your room, says Dad.

Maybe he's mad at me now for leaving school. I go to my room and lie down on my bed. I think about how the piece of Styrofoam will always be there in that spot.

Mother is not buried anywhere. She wanted to be cremated like Uncle Alexander. That means now they are ashes, but I don't believe it.

We buried Grandmother Bernie.

Grandmother Bernie died first. Then Uncle Alexander. Then Mother.

After dinner, Dad says he's taking me away. He says that he and I are going to the summerhouse. We can stay as long as we need to.

I thought you were going to take over that music theory class, Cass says.

I decided not to, says Dad. I have to finish the book.

Fine with me, Leo says and he walks away.

I talked to Mrs. Franklin, says Dad. She can make dinners and check in on you.

Mrs. Franklin lives next door. Her kids are all grown up and gone.

Cass hits the table with the side of her fist.

You make everything worse, she says to Dad and then locks herself in the bathroom to smoke.

I stand outside the door and I can smell her cigarettes. When she comes out, I follow her over to where Dad's still sitting at the table.

You don't know what you're doing, Cass says to Dad. She turns around and I'm behind her.

Sebby is fine, Cass says, you don't need to take him away. She grabs me and pushes me in front of Dad. She tells me to tell Dad that I'm fine.

I'm fine, Dad, I say.

Dad shakes his head.

Now I go into the bathroom and lock the door. The bathroom is cloudy with smoke. Cass puts out her cigarettes in the toilet water and they float around in there like dead fish. I flush them away. Then I sit and think. If Dad takes me to the summerhouse, I won't have to go to school.

Someone knocks on the door.

Sebby, come out, Dad says. If you don't want to go we don't have to.

I come out.

I'll go, I say.

We haven't been to the summerhouse since Uncle Alexander died there.

That's almost three years ago now, Dad tells me. Dad talks a lot in the car. He says I have to keep him company so he doesn't get sleepy.

Do you think Cass is mean? I ask Dad.

Dad says no. He says that he's done lots of mean things.

I'll tell you, he says, the meanest thing I ever did was walk a cow up the stairs in my grandmother's farmhouse. They couldn't get it back down. I knew they wouldn't be able to, because I'd read that a cow will walk upstairs, but not down. They had to lower the cow off the upstairs deck with a crane and the whole time that cow was crying like a baby. It was horrible.

You're nice to me, I say.

That's easy, Dad says. You know, he tells me, we're going to be okay. A break will be good for us.

I remember the summerhouse is small and white and has a dock that goes out to the ocean. It's where Mother and Uncle Alexander grew up.

Dad says we'll probably have to clean up a little bit because nobody's been living there and it hasn't been rented out since last summer.

I look in the bag of snacks that Cass packed for me. I pick out a red box of raisins.

Dad, I say, you know what?

I keep looking at the lady on the raisin box.

What? Dad asks.

Mother kind of looked like this lady, I say, and I show him the box. She looks bright, like she's standing with the sun shining on her.

You think so, he says.

I nod.

Dad points out ahead. His eyes are blinking fast and he has to clear his throat before he talks.

Look, he says, the ocean.

In the kitchen, there's a picture of Mother ice-skating with Cass and Leo. Leo's a baby in a blue hat. His head looks too big. Mother and Cass are pushing him around the ice in his stroller. I pick up the picture and look at it so close that it just blurs into colors. Then I put it back down where it was.

I open all the cabinets. There are white plates and white bowls and tall, clear glasses. The drawers are mostly empty. In the top drawer I find Scotch tape and two batteries, a red colored pencil and a stone shaped like a fish, painted orange with a black dot for an eye. I pick up the orange fish. It's cold. I touch it to my face and then I put it back where it was.

At home, sometimes I thought Mother was hiding here in this house.

I pick up the phone that's hanging on the wall and listen to the fast beeping sound.

Hello, I say and then hang up.

I look for Dad. He's outside by the car with his hands full of all our stuff.

Sebby, come help, he says. Dad gives me the light bags to carry.

We make a big pile in front of the stairs.

I'm starving, Dad says, we have to get some groceries.

It's dark when we come back to the house. I go around and turn on all the lights I can find. Some of the lightbulbs are burned out, but Dad says we'll worry about that tomorrow.

Sebby, Dad calls to me from the kitchen. We should eat, he says.

Dad bought us hot dogs for dinner. He puts four of them in the microwave. It hums a fuzzy sound like a radio between stations. I remember Mother told me I used to like listening to the sound of white noise on the radio. It put me to sleep when I was a baby.

I stand close to watch the hot dogs cook.

Get away from there, Dad says, it'll give you cancer.

When Dad takes the hot dogs out, I wonder if they have cancer in them now. We eat the hot dogs plain, because Dad didn't buy buns or ketchup.

Tastes good, I say.

Dad laughs at me. He eats his hot dogs fast.

I'm tired, he says and stretches his arms up.

I don't know how he's tired when everything here is new and we haven't looked at all of it yet.

I'll go make a fire, says Dad. He goes to the other room with the fresh wood we bought.

I stop eating my cancer hot dog and look at the picture of Mother ice-skating with Cass and Leo. Mother's laughing and you can see her pretty teeth. They're so white.

Sebby, Dad calls for me again.

The fire's burning and he's lying in his sleeping bag. Mine's rolled out next to his.

We'll clean up in the morning, says Dad.

I lie down and take off my glasses. In my room, I set my glasses on the table next to my bed. Here, I don't know where's a safe place, so I put them back on.

Dad, I say quietly. He doesn't answer.

I can't fall asleep with the fire so bright and lights still on all over the house.

Mother was going to have a baby girl. We were going to name her Sara Rose. Two names like one.

I think of the baby's name like this: Share a rose. Sir, a rose. Is air a rose.

I never got to meet her. She's with Mother. She was there on the night that Mother died and now they're still together.

Dad's not in his sleeping bag anymore when I wake up.

Dad, I say as loud as I can.

In here, he says.

He's up on a ladder in the kitchen, pulling spiderwebs off the ceiling. The ceiling's dark wood and the spiderwebs are like thin clouds.

I need to write a letter, I tell Dad.

Just a minute, Sebby, he says.

I stare up and watch him work. In my head, I count to sixty.

Dad, I say, it's been a minute.

He comes down the ladder and looks at me.

A letter? he asks.

I nod.

Dad starts looking through all the drawers in the kitchen. He brings me the red colored pencil and two dirty pieces of white paper that both have a bunch of numbers added up on one side and nothing on the other side.

This is all we've got for now, he says.

I lie down on my stomach and start coloring over all the numbers until I make that whole side red. Then I turn the paper over. I think first about what I want to write because the red pencil doesn't have an eraser.

I write, Dear Katya. It takes me a long time to think of what else to put. Then I write, I'm sorry that I bit you and made you cry. I draw her a picture of a boat floating in the middle of an ocean to fill up the rest of the page. Above the boat, I draw a big red sun in the sky. Since there's another piece of paper, I write another letter.

Dear Ms. Lambert,

    I want to write you a letter.

    Mother grew up in this white house. I like the white house, but there are closets and drawers that I still need to look in. I have to see where everything is so when I close my eyes, I can see it all in my head. I don't know what room was Mother's room.

    Here is a picture of the house. Do you like it?

Bye, Sebby

The shed in the backyard is the same white box shape as the house, only smaller. I slide open the door and inside is dark with a smell of cold leaves and gasoline. I like the gasoline smell. It's a metal taste all the way in the back of my throat.

I find a lawn mower, a rusty toolbox, and a plastic Christmas tree. Against the back wall, there's a yellow bike with purple streamers in its handlebars.

I reach my hand out, but I have to step closer to touch the bike. It feels wet-cold.

In here is the kind of quiet that makes you want to touch something or make something move.

Really fast, I grab on to the bike's handlebars and push it out of the shed. Then I let go.

The bike falls sideways on the grass and a bell on the handlebar rings.

I run away, back inside the house.

In the kitchen, through the window above the sink, I can see the shed and the yellow bike with the handlebars twisted, pointing up at the sky. I can see the dock, too, the one that goes all the way out to the ocean, but you can't walk on it because it's blocked by an orange and white road sign that says, NOT SAFE.

Dad wanders around the house with his cup of coffee.

All day, he's been walking around like this, moving furniture, setting up everything. I follow him to the room at the very end of the hall upstairs.

You can sleep in here, Dad says. It used to be your grandfather's study.

We look at the room together from the doorway.

Dad put my blue and yellow sheets on the small bed that's pushed into a corner. On the wall there's a painting of a sad old man holding a dead bird in his hand.

What do you think? Dad asks.

It's okay, I tell him. I'm looking at the painting, so Dad looks at it, too.

Your Grandpa Chuck loved birds, Dad says. He had a pigeon coop in the backyard.

Oh, I say.

I go downstairs, back to my sleeping bag in the fireplace room, where I left my letters for Katya and Ms. Lambert. Katya's letter has turned softer from all the red coloring on it. I touch it to my face and breathe in the pencil smell.

Dad, I call to him. I want to mail my letters.

I listen to his feet coming downstairs. He's wearing socks, so his feet make a quiet thump on each step.

Dad gives me money to buy stamps and envelopes. He says I can walk into town by myself because it's not far. It's the same way we walked yesterday to buy groceries.

The post office is painted brown, he says. You'll find it. Please, Sebby, says Dad, I need some quiet.

But we've been quiet all day.

Go ahead, Dad says.

I step outside and then turn around to look at him.

I'm just going to lie down, Dad says, I'll feel better by the time you get back.

I walk fast. I'm watching my feet on the sidewalk, but I have to look up if I want to find the post office, so I slow down and look.

I see the brown building with a sign that says UNITED STATES POST OFFICE in blue letters. It's right next to a park that has four swings, a merry-go-round, and a jungle gym with a clown's head on top. The clown is smiling and has a black hat with a yellow flower on it. I don't like him, because his big eyes are looking at me.

I run to the glass doors and go inside the post office.

Hello, says the lady behind the counter.

I take Dad's money out of my pocket and hand it to her. She has dark pink fingernails and lips. When she smiles at me, I see some of the pink from her lips is smudged on her teeth that are yellow, not white like Mother's teeth.

I want stamps and envelopes, I tell her.

She keeps smiling.

Well, she says and puts Dad's money away in the cash register. I can give you ten stamps and a pack of twenty envelopes.

Okay, I say.

Then she gives me back a handful of change and puts the stamps and envelopes in a bag for me to carry. Outside, I sit down on the sidewalk to get the letters ready and when I look at one of the blank envelopes, I know I can't mail the letters because I don't have the addresses.

Now the only thing to do is walk all the way back to the white house. I think about the yellow bike from the shed. Dad said he'd help me fix it up. I walk slowly with Katya's letter in my hand. Even though I'm by myself, I pretend like Katya's watching me. I do a skip-walk for her.

Dad's taking another nap.

I can't find any scissors, so instead I look for a knife in the silverware drawer. I pick the biggest one. It has wood on the handle part where you hold it.

I take the knife outside with me to the yellow bike. I know purple streamers make it look like a girl bike, so I try to cut them off. I have to cut one at a time and when I'm done, there's still short pieces of purple poking out like stupid, purple whiskers.

Wind blows the streamers all over the front steps and the grass and everywhere. I just let them go.

Since I don't know how to ride, I hold on to the handle-bars and take the bike for a walk with me. The faster I go, the louder the bike squeaks, so I have to walk slowly.

Hey, says a voice from somewhere up high.

I look around. In a window all the way at the top of a tall, blue house, I see a boy waving.

Hey, the boy says again. He leans forward so his head's all the way out the window. I can tell that he doesn't have a shirt on.

Listen to this, he says and he plays a harmonica. The way he plays doesn't sound like a song to me.

Then the boy goes away and the window's empty. I stand there watching, waiting for him to come back. I count slowly in my head. If I get to sixty, I'm going to leave.

I count all the way to thirty-four and then the boy comes back to the window with a girl. She waves at me and this time I wave back.

The boy plays his harmonica the same way—not like a song.

Then he says, What's your name?

I don't want to tell him my name, so I don't say anything.

Hey, the boy says, what's your name?

The girl waves at me again. She's wearing a red shirt and she has red curly hair like a clown.

What's your damn name? the boy asks.

I start to walk away and push the bike along with me. I hold on tight to the handlebars. I hold on so tight that my hands go white and I can't feel my fingers. I keep looking back at the boy in the window.

He throws a shoe and it lands behind me. It's a small, white buckle shoe.

My shoe, my shoe, yells the girl with red hair.

I walk a little bit faster and the bike squeaks louder. I want to drop it and run, but my hands won't let go.

I run with the bike screaming at me. I run all the way back to the white box house, where purple streamers are still blowing all over the grass. I must not have closed the door all the way because now it's blown open.

I pull the bike up the steps with me, into the house, and I slam the door shut with my foot. Then my hands let go of the handlebars and the bike flops over onto the floor.

Dad, I yell.

In here, he says.

Dad's sitting at the kitchen table with a big bottle of Coke and a box of pizza.

I'm cold and my teeth are chattering. I want to go sit on Dad's lap.

Don't slam the door like that, he says, you'll give me a heart attack.

I tell him, Sorry.

I ordered us a pizza, he says.

Dad, I say. I try to tell him what happened. I got really cold, I say.

He stands up and walks over to me. His face looks different, skinnier, because his beard is shaved-off.

Sebby, says Dad and I start crying. Dad pulls me closer. He rubs my shoulders with his hands to make me warm.

You're okay, Dad says and he walks me over to the sink. Dad holds my hands under the warm water. My teeth stop chattering and I feel better.

Shhh, Dad says, you're okay.

I look up at him.

Your glasses are filthy, he says. How can you even see out of those?

I shrug and let him take my glasses. He washes them for me. When he reaches up for a dish towel, there isn't one, so he pulls off his gray T-shirt and dries my hands with it and then dries my glasses. His chest has curly black hair. Down low on his stomach there's a scar that's whiter than his skin and it's from having his appendix taken out.

Dad holds up my glasses and looks through the lenses.
Much better, he says and puts them back on me.

How's that? he asks.

The yellow bike squeaks, I tell him. I don't like the sound.

I'll look for something to spray it with, Dad says. He rolls
his gray shirt into a ball and then sets it down on the counter.

Your beard is gone, I tell him.

I know, says Dad and he touches his hand to his smooth
face.

Listen, after dinner, you need to take a hot bath, he says,
and no more going outside without your coat.

I have a puffy green coat for when it's cold, but I don't
like to wear it. It zippers all the way up to my chin and feels
too tight around my neck.

Dad opens the pizza box and lets the steam out. He pours
two glasses of Coke—one for him, one for me.

We don't need plates, Dad says, they'll just be more dishes
to wash.

So we eat out of the box.

I don't know if I should drink my Coke or not. I only take
two sips. Mother didn't let me drink Coke because then I
wouldn't grow, but she drank it in the morning when she woke
up. She put chocolate syrup in her Coke and every time before she took a sip, she stirred it up with a long spoon and the
spoon made clinking noises against her glass. I liked to stir it
for her and make the clinking noises myself. Sometimes she
let me have a sip. Leo said that Coke is bad because it has acid
in it. I can't remember the name of the acid, but Leo said that

it was bad for Mother to drink. Mother said that Leo was being silly, but Leo said he was telling the truth and he put a nail at the bottom of a glass and then he filled it up with Coke. After four days, the nail really was gone, but Mother still drank her Coke in the morning. Leo said that when there's an accident on the highway and they need to clean the blood off the road, they use a big bottle of Coke. That's enough, Mother told Leo and then he stopped.

In the bath, I lie all the way back so my ears are underwater. There's the sound of my heart beating and the humming sound of blood going through me. Drips from the faucet land in the bath. They're loud and heavy sounding.

I remember, at the swimming pool I didn't want to put my head under. The swimming teacher said I had to. I held on to my blue foam kickboard. I liked to bite into the blue foam when she wasn't looking. The swimming teacher put on her frog goggles that said SPEEDO across the noseband in white letters and she showed me how to go under. I watched the bubbles coming up out of her nose.

I wouldn't do it.

Mother helped me out of the pool and dried me off with one of the scratchy, white pool towels.

She whispered, That's okay, my son, you have years and years to put your head underwater. Her breath in my ear made me shiver. Mother held me close.

I try to hear Mother's voice now under the bathwater, but I can't. Her voice is gone. I sit up fast and slide forward and then back again, forward and then back again, and the water moves with me, like waves. When I stop sliding, the water keeps moving and it pushes me back and forth, back and forth.

Dad comes in with a blue towel. It's my blue towel from home.

I found some WD-40 out in the shed, Dad tells me. I can spray the bike so it won't squeak.

Yes, I say.

Okay now, he says, let's get you out.

I don't want to stand up, because then I'll be cold, but Dad says it's time. He's still not wearing a shirt. I look at the place where his appendix came out.

Dad holds the towel, ready to wrap me up. I stand up fast and reach out with my finger to touch Dad's bumpy, white scar. I touch it, but I can't really feel anything because my finger is all shriveled from being in the water so long.

Will it be there forever? I ask Dad.

Yes, he says.

I wrote Mother a very important note and taped it to the mirror in her bathroom.

The note said:

To Mother,
    Please wake me up. I want to go with you.
                                        From, Sebby

I was sitting on the floor in my room, making a tower out of blocks. Mother sat down and helped me build the tower. She gave me back the note.

I miss you too, sweetheart, Mother said. Then she left.

I thought about how she wasn't alone because there was the baby, Sara Rose, in her stomach. Sara Rose was a part of her, listening to the outside through Mother's skin. They were together at night, when Mother ran.

A big envelope comes in the mail from Ms. Lambert. I like how my name looks in her perfect, teacher handwriting. Up in the corner is Ms. Lambert's name with the school address underneath. I'm happy because now I have a place to send my letters.

Inside the envelope is a packet of homework that I have to do, so I sit at the kitchen table with my red pencil. I skip the fraction page and turn to the part where I have to look at the sentences and underline nouns. I know nouns are people, places, or things, and that makes them easy to find.

The phone rings and I jump. I run over to where it's hanging on the wall and pick up.

Sebby? says Cass's voice.

You scared me, I tell her.

Sorry, she says. How's Dad? Is it cold there?

I'm wrapping the phone cord around and around my finger. Teacher sent me homework to do, I tell her.

That's good, Cass says. Is it snowing? she asks.

No, I tell her.

It's snowing here, she says.

Since I know I can walk to the post office by myself, I leave
Dad and the bike in the white house and I go. I'm wearing my
green coat and it's so puffy I can't feel the envelope that I
put in the front pocket. I have to keep touching it and then
I know it's still there. The envelope has the letters for Katya
and Ms. Lambert and also my homework page with the nouns
underlined.

I stop when I get close to the blue house and listen. I know
that the boy without a shirt and the girl with red hair live inside
of it, but they don't know which house is mine. The blue house
is quiet. Its windows are dark and empty. I walk a little closer
and stop again. On the ground, there's the white shoe that was
supposed to hit me.

I keep walking, but then I turn around and go back to the
white shoe. I look at it and what I think of is the picture of the
old man holding a dead bird in his hand. I know I can't leave
the shoe all alone, so I hide it inside of my coat, and cross my
arms tight. I walk faster now because what if someone's watching me from a window? I look back at the blue house again
and then I run.

At the post office, I don't need to go inside because they
have a blue mailbox in front. Through the glass doors, I can
see the same lady working behind the counter. She sees me
and waves without smiling and that's good. I don't like how
her teeth look when she smiles at me.

I take the envelope out of my pocket and look at how I wrote Ms. Lambert's name and Katya's name and also the address where my school is. Maybe when Katya reads my letter she'll be my friend again.

I pull on the handle and the blue mailbox opens up like a mouth. Really fast, I reach inside and drop the envelope. It doesn't make any sound when it lands. I try to look inside the mailbox, but it's just dark, like the letters are already gone.

On the way home, I don't want the shoe anymore, because it belongs to the girl with red hair. Even if the shoe is sad like a dead bird, it was still mean to take it away and I want to put it back. I walk fast all the way to the blue house. I know where the shoe was and I can put it in the same spot so nobody will know that I took it.

I find the spot and stand right there and then let the shoe fall out of my coat. The heel clicks when it hits the cold cement and makes a quick, hollow sound. I keep looking at the white shoe on the ground and I can't believe that it could make a sound at all. I want to pick up the shoe and drop it one more time to see if it will make that noise again. I can't, though. I have to run away before someone sees me.

I run and the air is cold on my cheeks. I can feel the cold inside my head and it stings, like there's ice behind my eyes. My head hurts every time my feet land on the ground, so I have to stop running. I take soft steps and that feels better. In the back of my head I can hear the sound of my heart beating. My heart is so loud that the whole inside of my body is filling up with sound.

In the morning, I go outside and the yellow bike is gone. I know who took it. I sit down on the front steps and wait for the boy from the blue house.

I decide I don't really care if he keeps the bike, because it's ugly and I don't know how to ride it. When the boy comes back, I'll tell him that I don't care. Then I'll go inside and lock the door so he'll have to go away. I know what to do.

I can hear the boy screaming at me before he comes around the corner. Then I see him. He's wearing just the hood part of his coat, so the rest of it flies behind him like a cape.

What's your name?! the boy screams. What'syourname, what'syourname, what'syourname! he screams and he rides the yellow bike toward me.

His sister is running after him and she's also screaming, What'syourname, what'syourname, what'syourname!

The boy rides right past me without stopping and the girl follows him. I look at her feet. She's not wearing the white shoes. She's wearing black high-top sneakers.

The boy turns around at the end of the street and comes toward me again. This time he stops in front of the white house and jumps off the seat so he's standing with one foot on each side of the yellow bike. His sister catches up with him.

You know how to talk or what? the boy asks me.

His sister's coughing from running so much. She bends

forward onto her knees, then sits down on the ground. She coughs without covering her mouth.

Do you talk? the boy asks me again.

Yes, I tell him.

Did you hear that? he asks his sister and she just nods her head.

Today the boy is wearing a shirt. It's gray with long sleeves. His coat looks funny now, hanging flat around his head. He's wearing shorts instead of pants even though it's cold outside. His shoes are tall, red cowboy boots that go all the way up to his knees. The girl stands up next to him so that I'll look at her, too. She's wearing jeans and a white coat. Her jeans are too short. I can see that she's wearing red socks.

Do you want your bike? the boy asks. His voice is louder again.

You can have it if you want, I tell him. I stand up because I'm ready to go back inside the white house and lock the door. Then the boy will have to go away.

Hey! he screams. He gets off the bike and pushes it over so that it lands hard on the ground and then kicks the front tire.

I don't want your damn, stinking bike, the boy says.

The girl copies him. She kicks the front tire and says, I don't want your damn, stinking bike.

Shut up, Shelly, the boy says and pushes her.

Who do you live here with? the boy yells at me. Then he starts coughing. He doesn't cover his mouth either.

My Dad, I tell him.

Do you want me to ring the doorbell and ask your dad what your dumb name is? he asks. His voice is quieter now.

No, I say. I sit back down on the front steps.

Well, then, he says and walks toward me. He looks back at his sister and puts his hand up so she doesn't follow him.

The boy keeps walking toward me and I don't know what to do.

My name is Sebby, I tell him to make him stop walking.

The boy stops and puts his hands in his pockets. Up close, he has freckles all over his cheeks and on his nose.

That's not a name, he says.

My whole name is Sebastian James Lane, I tell him.

The boy nods his head at me.

Okay, fine, he says, Sebastian James Lane. He says my name funny, like it's a fancy name.

I don't like how he says it.

My name is Jackson and that's Shelly, he says. He points at his sister and she stands up, but then he holds his hand out the same way as before and that means she has to stay where she is.

Nice to meet you, the boy says and puts out his hand for me to shake.

I shake it and then he walks away.

Hey! the girl yells at me, how come you wear glasses all the time?

So I can see more, I tell her

The boy turns around to look at me.

See ya, he says. Next time you don't have to be such a jerk.

Dear Ms. Lambert,

A long time ago, I fell out the window and I was okay. I was thinking about falling and what it would be like and then it happened.

There's a boy here named Jackson and a girl named Shelly. I had to tell them my name and now maybe they will be nice to me.

I have a dead Grandpa Chuck who liked pigeons. Do you think that's weird to like pigeons? I don't like any birds, because when I see one then I think something bad is going to happen.

Mother saw a bird in the white frosting ceiling and I could see it, too. After that, Mother was sad all the time. I used to stare at the bird and wish for Mother to be happy again. When Mother died, the bird was gone. I couldn't find it. I thought maybe the bird took Mother away.

Bye, Sebby

I look in the upstairs closet to find Grandpa Chuck's box. I want to know about pigeons and why they are good.

All the way up on the top shelf, I see a box that says CHUCK in capital black letters. I get a chair to stand on so I can reach, but the box is too heavy for me to pull down.

What I want to do is hide in the closet. I think it would be okay to hide for just a little bit, so I go in and pull the door shut almost all the way. Then I sit down and scoot to the back. I want to see if Dad will find me, but then I would be hiding for too long.

Inside the closet, it smells like outside. It smells like the cold-air smell of winter coats. I like being in the dark, but I have to remember I can only hide for a little bit.

I know Dad is upstairs where I am, because I can hear his music now. It sounds soft, like a lullaby. It's the Mamas and Papas song about a man who stands in his window and watches girls walking through the canyon. Mother told me that New York City is like a canyon, because the buildings are so tall.

The closet light wakes me up.

Dad says hello. His eyes look red and sleepy. He asks me what I'm doing and his voice sounds mad at me.

Sebby, he says, do not hide from me again. Then he goes away.

I stay in the closet. I'm lying on a brown box. The box is old and soft. It says Mother's name, LOUISE, and also Uncle's name, ALEXANDER.

I should go downstairs to my sleeping bag because I'm tired and I don't want to know what's in the box right now. But, I open one of the top flaps, put my hand inside, and pull out a red piece of paper that's written on with black crayon. The writing is messy and this is what it says:

> *Cass Love Mom*
> *Mom Cass Love*
> *Love Mom Cass*
> *Mom Love Cass*
> *Cass Mom Love*
> *Love Cass Mom.*

At the bottom of the red paper, in pencil handwriting, it says, Cass, age five, December 12, 1978.

I put the red paper back in the box and I think about going downstairs, but I don't. I reach in the box and take out a picture of a birthday cake that says HAPPY BIRTHDAY LOUISE. The picture is black-and-white. I count and there are fifteen candles on the cake. Mother's not in the picture. You can only see the cake.

I leave the picture and go downstairs. Dad's already asleep and the fireplace room is dark except for the fire. I like listening to how the wood pops when it burns.

I think about how Mother was fifteen and we were not with her. I was hiding somewhere, watching her, but I was not really me yet. Dad was somewhere, too, but he was not with Mother. He didn't know her until she was sixteen and went to Sandy's Escape and together they heard the song "Satisfaction." Uncle Alexander was probably there with Mother and Grandmother Bernie and Grandpa Chuck, too. Mother knew them before she knew Dad, Cass, Leo, and me. Now Mother is with only the baby, Sara Rose.

I can't fall asleep because I know what I want is to remember everything Mother did.

FAVORITES

In the morning, I find Dad upstairs in the room where he's supposed to sleep. The bed is set up with his yellow sheets and blankets that have tiny blue flowers all over them. I think it's not right for Dad to sleep with all those blue flowers since flowers are for girls and he doesn't sleep with Mother anymore.

Dad's watching TV, but the picture on the screen is not moving and I don't hear any sound.

What channel is this? I ask Dad.

It's a video, he says, I found it in the closet last night. I got down your grandfather's box of bird stuff, too, he says.

The picture on the TV screen is just a girl sleeping in a white bed.

That's Cass, Dad says and nods at the screen.

The sleeping girl's face looks so much softer than Cass's face. I don't think it's really her.

She's maybe twelve or thirteen here, Dad says.

What's she doing? I ask.

Sleeping, says Dad.

Oh, I say.

I'd just bought my first video camera, Dad says. He's talking and watching the TV screen. Cass wanted me to tape her early in the morning before she woke up so that she could see what she looked like when she was sleeping.

Why? I ask.

I don't like watching Cass sleep.

I don't know, Dad says, just curious, I guess.

Dad, I say.

He looks at me for a second.

Yeah, he says and then looks back at the screen.

Is Cass like Mother? I ask.

In some ways, yes, says Dad. I guess I don't know what you mean exactly.

I mean she doesn't look right with her eyes closed and her face empty like she's not feeling anything, but I don't say that. I don't say anything.

In the hallway, I look through the box of Grandpa Chuck's bird stuff and find something to ask Dad about.

What's this? I ask. I'm holding up an X-ray of a bird with its wings spread out.

Dad doesn't answer, so I go over to him and pull on the leg of his gray sweatpants.

Just a second, Dad says and stands up. He reaches forward to push the big button that turns off the TV.

That's an X-ray, Dad says. He stretches up tall so his white T-shirt goes up and I can see his stomach with the rubbery scar from where they took his appendix out.

Who is it in the X-ray? I ask.

It's Butch, your grandfather's favorite pigeon, says Dad. Butch got sick and your grandfather called a special bird doctor all the way out in New Hampshire or someplace and paid for the guy to fly here with all his equipment. The doctor said he couldn't guarantee anything. He was a weird guy. He talked slow and had a tiny, funny mustache.

Dad stops and rubs his face with his hands, then says, The

doctor took that X-ray to see inside Butch's lungs. Turns out Butch had pneumonia.

Dad points to light gray spots on the X-ray. See, he says, that's all fluid.

I touch one of the light gray spots and keep my finger there to cover it up.

What happened? I ask Dad.

Well, he says, the doctor helped your grandfather set up a sickroom for Butch. A cardboard box with a utility lamp clamped above to keep him warm. He survived in there for almost two weeks, I think.

I put the X-ray of pigeon Butch back in the box and close the lid. I don't want to know how light gray spots of fluid got inside his lungs. I don't like to look at the bird's body of bones and know he's dead.

I'm hungry, I tell Dad.

Okay, says Dad, we'll have to go out.

Can we drive? I ask.

We haven't driven anywhere since we came here. It's been days and days.

I guess so, Dad says.

I follow him downstairs and we get ready to go. Without any socks, Dad puts on his boots and laces them up really slowly. He keeps holding out the loose ends of the laces to make sure they're both the same length. I watch him and in my head I start to count. I count as fast as I can.

All right, Dad says and he looks up at me.

I can't stop counting in my head.

Dad finds the car keys in the pocket of his gray coat.

Outside, he keeps feeling around in all his pockets like he's missing something. He pulls out a red pack of sugarless gum and also a five-dollar bill.

Look, he says.

I look, but I don't say anything because I'm still counting.

You want a piece? Dad asks.

Then I have to stop counting to answer. We're standing by the car and Dad's looking at me, waiting.

Okay, I say. I'm not counting now, but I can still feel the numbers moving fast through my head. The numbers make my foot tap.

What are you doing? Dad asks.

Nothing, I say and we get in the car.

I put the piece of gum in my mouth. I used to not like this kind because it tasted too spicy, but now I like how it makes the inside of my mouth feel hot.

We drive into town and after we pass by the post office, then everything's new. Dad parks in front of a brown restaurant with a sign that says Mitchell's.

I haven't been here in years, Dad tells me.

We get out and I run around to Dad's side so I can lock the car. I like listening to the clicking sound.

The restaurant is loud inside. I follow Dad to a booth. We have our own window, but there's nothing to see really, except for all the cars parked in a row. Our car is parked in the middle and I think that's a good place for it to be.

A tall waitress brings us water. She's wearing a short, black skirt so you can see almost all of her long, skinny legs. She asks Dad if we're ready to order.

You want pancakes? Dad asks me.

I nod yes. The waitress looks funny like how flamingos look funny. On her long neck she's wearing a gold cross necklace.

Dad orders pancakes for me and also eggs over easy with well-toasted toast for him.

The waitress goes away and Dad rubs his forehead with both hands like he's tired already. Then he looks out the window. He's sad for Mother and sad for himself. I know he's sad all the time and I heard Cass say that maybe he'll never feel better.

I slide forward off the booth and go under the table. Dad doesn't tell me not to, so I lie down on the floor and look up. There's one name scratched into the wood. Rachel, it says.

I take my red piece of gum out of my mouth and stick it next to the name Rachel. I tell myself to remember how I lay under the table and stuck my piece of gum there. If I tell myself to remember something like that, then it stays in my head.

I remember I locked myself in the bathroom at home and lay down on the floor. It was my birthday and I was wearing my new spaceman pajamas that Mother gave me. I took the piece of grape gum I was chewing out of my mouth and stuck it all the way at the back of the cabinet under the sink. The gum was my birthday present from Leo. He gave me ten packs of grape bubblegum and Mother said it would ruin all my nice new teeth. I had three new teeth on the bottom, but I still had my baby teeth on top. I stuck my piece of grape gum in the back of the cabinet and I told myself to remember lying down there on the floor on my birthday and it worked, so that's how I know how to make myself remember.

Dear Ms. Lambert,

I do know what happened to Mother. I wasn't there, but I was.

I was sleeping and I could see Mother running in the dark. She was holding her stomach. There weren't any cars, so she was running in the middle of the street.

I want to remember everything that Mother did, but if I try too hard, then I'm thinking, and thinking is not the same as remembering.

Bye, Sebby

Dad's upstairs when the doorbell rings and he doesn't come down so I have to answer it. I only open the door a tiny bit and I can see it's the boy, Jackson, with his sister standing behind him.

Come on, open up, Jackson says.

I open the door a little more, but I stand in the open space so that he can't come in.

What do you want? I ask him.

We came to find out what you're going to be for Halloween, says Jackson.

I don't say anything. I look down at Jackson's feet. He's wearing his red cowboy boots and also jean shorts. I can see his knees are purply red from the cold.

I'm going to be a street-fighting ninja, Jackson says.

I'm going to be Robin, says his sister.

She wants to be Robin even though I'm not going to be Batman this year, Jackson says. It's stupid.

Jackson, you shut up, his sister says. She has big, watery eyes.

What are you going to be? Jackson asks me again.

I don't know, I tell him.

Sebby, Dad's voice says from behind me.

I turn around and look at him at the top of the stairs. He's wearing his white T-shirt and his gray sweatpants with one sweatpant leg pushed up around his knee.

Who's there? he asks.

I open the door more so he can see Jackson and his sister.

Oh, Dad says and walks away.

That's your Dad? Jackson asks.

If you take your glasses off, you could be Batman, his sister says to me. She moves closer so she's standing next to Jackson and not behind him anymore. Her face has freckles all over it and her lips are chapped. They're chapped because she keeps licking them. She looks sad with her big, watery eyes.

No, I tell her. I don't really know anything about Batman.

Nobody wants to be Batman and Robin with you, says Jackson.

Then she kicks him hard and low on the leg. Jackson pushes her away with one hand.

Cut it out, he tells her.

Did you see *Batman Returns*? she asks.

I shake my head.

Are you going to be anything or what? Jackson asks me.

Maybe, I say.

I want him to go away now. I don't care about Halloween.

You got anything in there you could wear that's scary? asks Jackson.

I shrug.

You're weird, his sister says to me and then she licks her lips. Her bottom lip is cracked in the middle and it's bleeding now.

You at least got a white sheet, Jackson says. You could be a ghost.

Okay, I tell him.

Come on, his sister says and she pulls on Jackson's arm.

Jackson shakes his arm to make her let go.

Come on, she says again.

Jackson pretends he can't hear her.

Well, he says to me. He keeps looking at my face, so I look away.

See ya, he says.

His sister's already walking away and he runs to catch up so he can walk in front.

Bye, I say.

Dad says I have to sit down at the table and do my homework. He brings me a glass of water and crackers for a snack.

How many pages do I have to do? I ask.

Two, says Dad.

I eat one cracker and then copy all the spelling words three times. On the fraction page, I make up answers.

Finished, I tell him.

That was quick, Dad says and he comes over to the table to see.

I show him the spelling words.

What about the math page? he asks.

No, I tell him.

Dad sits down and shows me how to draw fractions like pies with slices cut out. Then I can see them in my head and I know how they work. Dad stays with me and watches me do the problems.

Good, he keeps telling me. After I do the last one, he walks over to the refrigerator and looks inside. So, you know those kids? he asks.

They live in the blue house, I tell him.

Dad yawns. We should go to the store, he says.

Yes, I say, I need a white sheet because I'm going to be a ghost.

What are you talking about? asks Dad. He walks back over to me.

I want to be a ghost, I tell him, a ghost is scary.

Dad scratches the top of his head. His hair is messy and greasy.

Your mother is not a ghost, he says.

I know, I tell him, it's Halloween.

When? Dad asks.

Dear Ms. Lambert,

I want to tell you something.

The night she left, Mother woke me up. She said, Sebby, you have to hear this. On the tape, the man said, And now to sing this lovely ballad, here is Mama Cass. Mother stopped the music then to make it start over. She said, Listen, Sebby. If you listen carefully, you can hear Mama Cass clearing her throat. The song started over again and she asked me did I hear it and I did, so I said yes and Mother loved me then. She picked me up out of bed and held me. I love you, little boy, she whispered. Mother whispered close to my ear and she kissed my face. I put my head down on her shoulder and I loved her, too. We listened to the song and Mother whispered the words to me about saying good night and dreaming about each other.

After the song, she put me back in bed and stayed there with me until I fell asleep. In the morning I found a piece of paper folded up under my pillow. The paper had all the words of the song written on it.

Bye, Sebby

We don't have a plain white sheet, so Dad gives me one that's white with little yellow flowers all over it.

You can turn it inside out, he says, then we'll cut two holes for eyes.

I tell him that we don't have any scissors.

I'm going to the store, says Dad.

I follow him to the door.

I'll buy scissors, he says. Lock the door behind me.

Then he goes.

I stand over by the window and watch him walking away. He forgot to wear his coat.

I don't like the sheet because even on the white side, the yellow flowers show through and I know I'm going to look stupid. I leave the sheet there on the floor and I put on my puffy green coat.

Outside, it's windy and the trees are loud. All the leaves are blowing away. I walk slow and count my steps so I can know how many it takes to get to the blue house. I count all the way up to 203 and then I stop counting because it's cold and I want to run, so I run the rest of the way.

I knock on the door and wait. The girl, Shelly, answers.

Hello, she says. She's wearing a blue sweatshirt that has white sheep all over it except for one black sheep at the bottom.

I have a question, I tell her.

Then Jackson comes running to the door to see who it is. When he sees me, he pushes his sister out of the way.

What day is Halloween? I ask him.

He scrunches up his face at me.

You don't know? asks Jackson. He shakes his head. It's today, he says.

I think about how that means it has been a whole year since last Halloween. Mother was alive then and she dressed me up as a white cat, like the cat named Duncan that she had when she was a girl.

Go get ready, he tells me, I'll come get you when it's dark.

I'm waiting and waiting, but Dad is not coming home from the store and it's getting dark now. I keep sitting at the bottom of the stairs, watching the door and listening for Dad. I can't get up since I didn't turn on any of the lights and now everywhere inside the house is dark. I bite the inside of my cheek to taste the blood in my mouth and that makes me feel better.

This kind of dark is scary.

I like the dark inside closets because I know that it's light outside in the rest of the house. When Mother's head was hurting really bad, I used to help her cover all the windows in my room to make it dark, all the way black dark, and then we liked to sit in there together. I would keep my eyes closed and then open them and nothing changed because the dark was so dark it was like the dark inside of my head.

I know what I have to do. I have to cut the sheet with the knife and make eye holes, but I am stuck at the bottom of the steps. I bite the inside of my cheek again and I think about how Mother said that it's a bad habit and I should try not to do it.

The dark is everywhere. Sometimes I think I hear Dad coming and I wait for the door to open, but nothing happens. If Jackson comes and rings the doorbell now, I can't answer it because I'm not ready.

Then the door opens. Dad doesn't see me in the dark. Dad, I say and my voice scares him because he doesn't know I'm right here.

Jesus Christ, Sebby, Dad says and he turns on the light.

You took a long time, I tell him.

He doesn't say anything. Dad has two bags of groceries and I can see now that his face is red and sweaty from carrying them.

Did you buy scissors? I ask.

Oh shit, says Dad.

How are we going to cut the sheet? I ask and follow him into the kitchen.

We'll figure it out, he says.

But we don't have time, I say, because it's already dark and Halloween is right now.

Dad stops putting the groceries away. I watch him take a deep breath.

Bring me the sheet, says Dad.

When I come back, Dad's holding the big knife. He takes the sheet from me and cuts all the way around to make it shorter. He doesn't cut very straight, but that's okay since I think that makes it look scarier. Then Dad folds the sheet in half and he pokes two holes at the top for my eyes.

Here, he says, try it on.

It's a little bit long, but I like it.

Come over here, says Dad. He cuts off a piece from the leftover sheet and uses that like a scarf to tie around my neck.

Now the ghost costume stays on me and I can run and it won't fall off.

I run upstairs to the big mirror in the bathroom and I look at myself. I'm only kind of scary because you can see the yellow flowers through the sheet. Maybe outside in the dark you won't be able to see the flowers. I run around fast at first and then slower, like how a ghost moves, and I keep going back to the mirror to see what I look like again.

When the doorbell rings, I run downstairs to answer. Jackson is there in his black ninja costume with his ninja mask and I know his costume is better than mine.

Are you ready? Jackson asks.

Yes, I tell him.

We're only allowed to stay out for an hour, Jackson's sister tells me. I'm in charge of the time, she says and shows me the black watch on her wrist.

I nod, then look at her feet and see that she's wearing her white shoes. They're so white in the dark that her feet glow.

Come on, Jackson says and starts running.

I have to hold up the bottom of my sheet so I can run without tripping. It's hard to see because my glasses are getting foggy from my breathing. I can hear Shelly behind me. Her white shoes make loud clicking noises on the sidewalk.

We gotta get to the good street, Jackson tells me when he stops to catch his breath.

Okay, I say.

They give out whole big candy bars, he says.

Shelly catches up to us and starts to cry.

I can't go that fast, she says.

You should have gone out with Mom, Jackson yells at her.

She just sits down and cries with her hands covering her ears and pretends she can't hear anything.

None of the houses here have their lights on for Halloween. I don't know where we are. The dark is all over and it makes everything far away, like you can't touch anything and I think I could run and run and still it would be dark like this with nothing to touch.

I think of Cass, far away with Leo. In my head, I can't see them. I can only see our house from the outside and I know they are somewhere inside of it. Even though it's night, I think of Ms. Lambert at school, sitting on her desk in front of the class with one ankle crossed over the other. She takes her black-and-white Chap Stick out of her pocket and I watch how she puts it on. Katya's wearing her yellow sweater. I can see her standing alone in the dark on the grassy school field.

Shelly cries louder and she's kicking at Jackson so he can't get close enough to talk to her. I want Shelly to stop because out here the sound goes everywhere and everyone can hear us.

Shelly, please stop, I tell her. I'm leaning forward, close to her ear.

Shelly looks at me. Her face is red and wet.

I'm not getting up unless you go slower, says Shelly. Her voice sounds stuffy like she has a cold.

Fine, Jackson says, I hope you know you're a big baby.

I'm telling, Shelly says.

Go ahead, says Jackson and he grabs her arm to pull her up so she's standing. Then he starts running, still holding her arm and pulling her along.

I run again, too, and it's quiet except for the sound of our feet. Running in the dark feels like being alone. I have to keep up with Jackson or I will be lost. I'm breathing hard and the air hurts the back of my throat. My sheet keeps slipping down and then I almost trip.

Here! Jackson yells and he stops.

Down the street, the houses are big and lit up and there are other kids. We can walk now because we made it. Jackson still holds Shelly's arm and has to pull her.

The first house we go to has fake cobwebs all over it and plastic skeletons and spooky music playing out the windows. Kids come running down the front steps and they push past us on our way up. I stay close behind Jackson and Shelly. Another kid comes down the steps by himself. He's wearing one of those plastic costumes you can buy at a drugstore. He's supposed to be the beast from the cartoon movie *Beauty and the Beast*.

She's only got Raisinets left, he tells us.

Jackson doesn't say anything to him, so I don't either.

At the top of the steps, a woman with gray hair says, Boo. She's not wearing a costume really, but she has fuzzy cat ears on her headband.

We take her Raisinets and run back down the stairs.

At the next house we get Snickers.

These are the best, Jackson says. He opens his and takes a bite before he puts it in his bag.

Come on, he says with his mouth full.

Shelly holds up her watch in the light from the house and it says 8:37. That means an hour already passed. Shelly starts crying again, not loud like before, but soft and quiet.

You take her now, Jackson says and gives me Shelly's arm.

I try to pull her along.

Come on, Shelly, I say, walk.

Jackson's getting way ahead of us.

We have to go faster, I tell her. I pull her a little harder. Jackson's waiting for us in front of the biggest house at the end of the street.

We're not going to get any candy if you guys go that slow, says Jackson.

Sorry, I tell him.

This is all your fault, Shelly yells at him.

Jackson ignores her and I follow him up the steps to the front door. I have to pull Shelly along with me. At the top of the stairs there's a note that says PLEASE ONLY ONE EACH, and below it is a bucket. A little kid dressed like a pirate with an eye patch and a stuffed-animal parrot stuck on his shoulder reaches in and pulls out something like a ball.

What the hell is that? says a bigger kid with a bloody skeleton mask.

I think it's a real shrunken head, Jackson says.

A kid dressed up in a furry tiger suit throws up all over himself.

That's disgusting, someone says.

We all reach into the bucket at the same time to grab one of the balls. Then we run back down the steps fast and I don't even have to pull Shelly.

At the next house we get peanut M&M's and then we get Tootsie Pops and then Kit Kat bars and that's it, because a brown van in the street honks at us three times.

Jackson says, Oh crap, it's Mom.

Shelly grabs my hand and takes me with her to the van. Jackson comes behind us. Their mom doesn't say anything when we get in.

Are you mad, Mom? Jackson asks her. She looks at him with her eyes small and mean.

Jackson made us come here and he was pulling me and hurting me, Shelly says and starts crying again.

Jackson's mom drives and it's quiet except for Shelly's crying. The crying is okay now that we're inside the van and not out in the dark.

Jackson's mom pulls up in front of the white box house.

Here's your stop, she says.

I can't get the sliding van door open, so Jackson has to do it for me. He doesn't say anything. He just opens the door and I get out.

Dad's still sitting in the kitchen.

What're you doing? I ask him.

Huh, Dad says. He scratches his hand through his hair.

I take the weird ball thing out of my candy bag and put it down on the table in front of him.

What is it? I ask.

A pomegranate, says Dad.

I shrug. I don't know that word.

It's fruit, he says. You can eat it. He stands up and brings a plate and a knife back over to the table.

I watch how he cuts the pomegranate in half. Dad picks out a little red seed and eats it.

Try one, he tells me.

I can't eat in my ghost costume. I point to my mouth to show Dad there's no hole.

Here, I'll fix it, says Dad, but you have to take it off for a minute.

Dad pulls the sheet off me and then uses the pomegranate knife to cut a hole for my mouth. It leaves a stain on the sheet like blood.

That makes it scarier, Dad says. He helps me put the sheet back on and ties the scarf around my neck.

I don't really like how the inside of the pomegranate looks with so many little seeds, but I pick one out. It tastes kind of sweet and crunches when I chew.

See, Dad says, it's good.

So we keep picking out little seeds and eating them. Our fingers turn red. Dad laughs and I laugh, too.

Then the doorbell rings and I don't want to answer it. I think maybe it's Jackson's mom and she's going to tell Dad how we went really far away.

Who the hell could that be? asks Dad.

I don't move, so Dad stands up to go see who it is. He licks his fingers and wipes them off on his gray sweatpants before he opens the door.

Leo, Dad says.

Hi Dad, says Leo.

I run over to see him. His hair is longer and hangs down over his eyes.

Leo puts down his duffel bag and gives Dad a fast hug. I watch how Dad pats Leo on the back twice and then they step back to look at each other.

Leo, I say and he looks at me then.

What happened to you? Leo asks.

I'm a ghost, I tell him.

But your hands, he says.

My hands are messy from eating.

Sebby brought home a pomegranate, Dad says and I point to it over on the table.

Do you want some? I ask.

Nah, says Leo. He walks over to where I am and hugs me hard.

How you doing? he asks.

It's Halloween, I say.

I know, he says.

We're all standing in the kitchen now. Dad's rubbing his chin and it makes a scratchy sound because his beard is starting to grow back.

Well, Leo says to Dad, I was worried—I mean, you sounded weird on the phone. Leo puts his hands in his pockets and pushes them in as deep as they'll go.

I'm fine, Dad says. We're fine, he says and looks at me.

Leo nods.

Cass wants to know if you're planning to vote, says Leo. It's a big deal, Dad.

Can we talk about it tomorrow? Dad says. It's late.

A social worker came to the house, Leo says, to check on us. She wants to talk to you.

Fine, says Dad. He walks out of the kitchen and then stops to turn around. You can sleep upstairs in the empty bed, he says to Leo. Sebby insists on sleeping down here.

Dad puts up his hand and waves. Good night, he says.

So you're all right, Leo says to me.

I nod.

Leo puts his hand on my head.

Nice costume, he says.

In the morning, we have a cat.

Dad says that he woke up early and went for a walk down to the water. When he came home, the cat was waiting by the door and followed him inside. The cat is a yellowish white, big cat with long fur and green eyes. Dad says the cat is a boy. We can't feed him yet, because if he has a home then he will leave after a while to get food. So we are waiting to see if the cat goes home. I want him to stay, but Leo says the cat is a good-looking cat and probably has a home. I put my hand out and the cat lets me pet him.

I'm glad I went to the store yesterday, Dad says. He's making us eggs for breakfast. We have orange juice, too. Dad pours three tall glasses and Leo sets out the plates and silverware.

You know the Patriots are playing today, says Leo.

Oh, yeah, Dad says, I can bring the TV down. I don't know how good the reception will be.

Dad comes over with the frying pan. He tips it so the eggs slide off. He puts one egg on my plate and two on Leo's plate and then he goes back to the stove. He cracks open two more eggs.

You know, Leo tells Dad, Bush is saying it wasn't just unpatriotic for Clinton to protest the war. He's attacking him on moral grounds.

Dad turns around with the spatula in his hand. They're a bunch of politicians, he says, it's all about politics.

But Bush is so much worse, Leo says and tips back in his chair.

Either way, says Dad, it won't make all that much difference.

I feel the cat push against my legs under the table. I lean over and look at him. Dad says that the cat is like the color of champagne. I put my hand out and the cat pushes his face against my hand and rubs the side of his face on my arm. Then he lies down by my feet and I pet him some more.

You need to sit up and eat, Dad says. He comes over again with the frying pan and puts two eggs on his own plate.

I'm not hungry, so I take just a little bite of the white part of the egg. Then I poke the yellow part with my fork and watch how the yellow leaks out. I don't like how it looks, but I take another bite so Dad doesn't get mad.

I found a bike, I tell Leo. Can I show him? I ask Dad.

Please try to eat a little more, he says and looks at my plate.

I take two fast bites.

Can you finish your orange juice? he asks me. Another sip at least?

I take a long sip and then I show Dad the glass.

I think I put the bike back out by the shed, says Dad.

Let's go, I say to Leo. I stand up and pull on his shoulder.

All right, he says.

I run through the house to the back door and outside. There's the bike, leaning against the shed.

I remember that bike, Leo says, and walks toward me.

Is it a girl bike? I ask.

Leo shrugs. Looks all right to me, he says. His hair is kind
of curly now that it's longer.

Cass used to let me ride it sometimes, says Leo.

Why didn't Cass come, too? I ask.

She's still mad at Dad, Leo says.

I think of Cass smoking a cigarette, not talking to anyone.

I don't know how to ride, I tell Leo. I look at the bike,
not at him. I keep looking at the bike, but I know Leo's looking at me.

Leo walks up and grabs the bike by the handlebars. He pulls
it over to where I'm standing.

It's easy, Leo says.

I look at his hands on the handlebars. He has long, skinny
fingers. His hands are the same as Mother's. They're pretty,
girl hands. I look at Leo's face with his long hair covering over
his eyes.

You gotta get on, Leo says, so I do. He holds the bike steady
for me to get up on the seat.

Okay, says Leo, now just pedal and I'll hold on as long as
I can.

I pedal and I can feel Leo holding on. It's good that Leo's
here now to hold on to the back of the seat and help me learn
to ride. He has to run a little bit to keep up with me. Then he
lets go.

Leo says, You can fall—we're on the grass.

I don't want to fall. I want to stop, but I don't know how.
I take my feet off the pedals and drag them on the ground, but
I'm not stopping and then the bike tips over to the side.

It's okay, Leo says.

He comes over to me. I fell and my side hurts, but I don't hurt anywhere else.

See, Leo says, it's easy. He helps me get up and then picks up the bike. If you want to slow down, he says, you gotta push back on the pedals. Okay? he asks.

Okay, I say.

Leo holds the bike steady for me to get on the seat and then I pedal again. I can feel Leo holding on and then I can't feel him anymore, so I push back on the pedals like he told me to. I push back hard and that makes me fall.

My glasses are crooked and there's blood in my mouth. It's not a little bit of blood, like when I bite my cheek, but a lot of blood. I close my eyes. The grass is scratchy on my face.

You can't stop that fast, says Leo. His voice is close. He puts his hand on my back.

Come on, Sebby, he says, look at me.

I turn over. Leo wipes my mouth with his shirt. I can see how my blood leaves a red stain on his sleeve.

You're okay, he says and fixes my glasses. His hair is hanging down in front of his face. I reach out and push his hair back off his forehead.

You bit your lip, he tells me.

The grass smell is getting all over me. I want to go inside.

We'll take a break, he says and helps me up. He holds my hand and we walk to the house. You just bit your lip, he tells me.

Dear Ms. Lambert,

On the day that Mother was dead, I didn't cry. It was in the morning. Dad was sitting on the end of my bed when I woke up and I asked him, What are you doing? His face was red and his eyes were wet. There was light shining out of his eyes. Dad kept touching his hands to his face. He put his hand over his mouth and then both hands on his cheeks.

Dad said that Mother was gone, that she was dead. I was sleeping when it happened. All of us were sleeping.

Dad reached out his arms and touched his flat, cold hand to my cheek. Then he picked me up and carried me downstairs.

I'm sorry, Dad said, I'm sorry.

Dad put me down on the couch. I got up and walked back upstairs to my room. I sat on my bed and didn't move. I didn't cry. Then Cass came. She didn't say anything. I let her carry me downstairs. She sat on the couch and held me on her lap. When she let me go, I went back upstairs to my room.

Dad came and sat next to me on my bed. He told me to cry. He told me to let it out.

Cry, Dad said.

I didn't cry.

I wanted to be back in the trees where I was before I was me. I wanted to be up high again and then Mother would be right there below me. I wanted to watch her and keep watching her always.

Bye, Sebby

I'm sitting under the table in the kitchen with the new cat. He likes me to pet him on top of his head between his ears and also under his chin.

Leo's standing over at the counter making sandwiches for the game. He had to go to the store to buy ham and turkey and mayonnaise.

Don't get too attached to that cat, says Leo.

I don't say anything.

Dad has the TV set up downstairs for the game and I can hear him making a fire in the fireplace. I look at my hands petting the cat. I like my hands. They're not like Mother's hands and they're not like Dad's hands either. Maybe before my hands were mine, they were Grandpa Chuck's. I think of Grandpa Chuck's hands holding birds, touching bird feathers.

The cat looks at me when I pet him on the back, but when I pet his head, he closes his eyes and purrs. My shirt has green on it from the grass and the smell is kind of sweet and dirty.

You did really great on the bike, Leo says to me.

I don't think so.

Come on, he says, the game's going to start.

I keep petting the cat.

Are you hiding? asks Leo.

I'm not, I tell him.

Then come on, he says.

I try to pick up the cat, but he's big and doesn't want to come with me. He taps me away with his paw.

Here, Leo says and gives me two bags of barbecue chips to carry.

Dad's standing up, watching the TV when we come in.

I think it'll work fine, he says and then turns and walks over to the stairs.

Where you going? Leo asks him.

I don't like to watch, says Dad. He's holding on to the railing and looking up the stairs.

Since when, Leo says. He sets a plate of sandwiches down on the table.

It makes me nervous, says Dad.

Jesus fucking Christ, Leo says and sits down on the couch.

Dad lets go of the railing and just stands there at the bottom of the stairs, but then he comes back over and sits down next to Leo. I'm still holding the two bags of chips. I set them on the table.

Can you go get the bottle of Coke? Leo asks me. He already put three tall glasses on the coffee table.

I left it out by the fridge, says Leo.

You drink Coke now? Dad asks.

Leo shrugs.

I go back into the kitchen. The cat is still under the table and I crawl under to sit with him. If I stay here, Leo will get mad. The cat pushes his face against my hand because he's happy that I'm back, but I have to get up now or Leo will say I'm hiding. I pat the cat's back two more times and then get up.

The bottle of Coke is wet and sweaty-looking from being out of the refrigerator. It's heavy and makes my hands cold when I carry it to the other room. I set it down on the table and Leo reaches for it. I look at his hands again.

Leo twists off the cap and the bottle makes a fizzing noise. You want some? he asks me.

Okay, I tell him, so he pours me a glass, too.

I crawl up onto the couch that smells like dust and sit next to Dad. I sit close to him and he puts his arm around me. Dad's looking at the TV, but he keeps closing his eyes. He closes his eyes for a long time, like maybe he's thinking hard or trying to fall asleep.

Dad, Leo says loudly and Dad's eyes open.

You know, Leo says, I want to talk to you about the election.

Dad nods. He stares at the TV.

Bush started a war, Dad, says Leo, and people died.

I don't want Leo to talk right now. I look at Leo and I wish he would be quiet.

I know, Dad says. His voice is slow and quiet.

I remember the war from TV. There were lights that flashed in the dark and Cass said that the lights were bombs and people were dying.

If you know, Leo says, then why don't you vote?

Dad closes his eyes again but not for very long. When he opens his eyes he says, Because honestly, Leo, I don't care.

Leo pulls his hair back tight into a short ponytail, then lets it go. He doesn't say anything else to Dad and I'm glad about

that. I want Leo to go away now. I like him being here to show
me how to ride the bike, but not anymore if he's going to be
mean to Dad.

Here, Leo says and hands me one of the sandwiches.

I take it, but I'm not hungry. The dust from the old couch
makes me sneeze.

Bless you, says Dad with his eyes closed.

A piece of tomato falls out of the sandwich and lands on
my lap. I just leave it there.

Leo yells, GO GO GO! at the TV because the players are
doing something good.

I sneeze again.

Bless you, says Dad. He pulls his arm away from me, then
stands up.

Where are you going? Leo asks him.

To the bathroom, Dad says.

But they're about to score, says Leo.

I know, Dad says. He walks away.

I feel cold now without Dad and I sneeze again. I wipe my
nose on my arm. Leo looks at me.

Why don't you eat the damn sandwich? he asks. He picks
the tomato off my lap and puts it on the sandwich plate.

I'm not hungry, I say.

Leo watches the game. Come on! he yells at the TV and
then there's loud cheering because the players got points. Leo
stands up to stretch and chip crumbs fall off him.

What's the matter? he asks me.

I don't say anything.

If you don't want the sandwich, that's fine, says Leo. He grabs it from me and throws it back on the plate.

We watch the TV even though commercials are on now. I'm waiting for Dad. I think Leo is waiting for Dad, too, but Dad's not coming.

Leo stands up and walks over to the stairs. I try to listen to him going up, but the TV's too loud. I wipe my runny nose on the back of my hand. I don't like how my hand smells like the turkey sandwich. There are too many smells and the smells are making me sick.

I hear heavy feet running downstairs and Leo's back with his duffel bag over his shoulder.

I gotta get out of here, he says. But listen, you be good. I'll call soon, Leo says and puts his hand on my head.

Then he takes a bag of chips and the big bottle of Coke and he goes.

I know Dad's not coming back downstairs now, so I turn off the TV. I run over to my sleeping bag and drag it into the kitchen, under the table, where the cat is waiting for me.

I wake up with something heavy on me. I try to push my-self up and then the cat meows and I know it's the cat on my back. I feel the cat turn around in a circle and then lie down again. I don't move because I want him to stay. It's so dark in here. I lie flat with the dark all around me and the cat heavy and warm on my back, but the inside of my sleeping bag is all wet.

This dark is not the good, small dark like the dark inside of my head or the dark hiding in a closet—it's a big dark that I don't know and it scares me. I call for Dad. I have to yell louder and louder to make him hear me. The cat runs away and my back feels cold now. I'm crying because I wanted the cat to stay and Dad's not coming. Inside my sleeping bag, I take off my wet clothes.

The kitchen light turns on and there's Dad in the light that's so bright it's burning my eyes. I keep blinking and look-ing at Dad.

What're you doing? Dad asks. He walks over to where I am under the table and then squats down low.

I woke up, I tell him.

Okay, says Dad. He reaches out to pull me over to him.

I'm wet, I say.

Dad nods.

That's okay, he says, come here.

He leans close to me and I hold on to his shoulders so he can pull me out of the sleeping bag. I'm so cold. My teeth are chattering loud.

Where are your clothes? Dad asks, because I only have on my underwear.

I point to the sleeping bag. In there, I say.

Dad carries me upstairs to the room that was Grandfather's study and now is where I'm supposed to sleep. He puts me on the bed that has my blankets and sheets from home. My teeth are loud and I can't make them stop. I look at the painting on the wall of the old man holding a dead bird in his hand. The old man is Grandfather, I think.

Dad brings clean underwear and my spaceman pajamas and helps me put them on.

Thank you, I tell him. I bite my teeth together hard to make them quiet.

No problem, Dad says and tucks me into bed. He pulls the covers up high, all the way to my chin. I like how he does that.

You'll be okay in here, Dad says and he kisses my forehead. His face is scratchy.

I close my eyes because I don't want to look at the painting of the old man. I hear Dad click off the light when he goes, but I keep my eyes closed because the old man will still be there in the dark. I know what I have to do.

I make my eyes open, but I don't look at the old man, not yet. I look up at the ceiling that's low and gray in the dark. I push the covers away and cold air gets all over me. Then I look down at the wood floor, reach my feet down to touch my toes first and I'm standing up. I keep looking down and take steps to where I know the old man is. I take soft steps, but the wood floor creaks at me.

I walk all the way to the old man and then I look up at his face. His eyes with their fat, tired eyelids look at me. I put my hand out and touch his chalky cheek. I hold my hand there because I'm not scared of him. With my finger, I touch his fat eyelids, one and then the other. His eyelids feel the same as his cheek.

I turn around and I know he's looking at me, but that's okay. I run back to bed and jump in fast. I pull the covers back over me and I can close my eyes now. The covers are cold and heavy. I have to wait for them to get warmer. I rub my feet together.

In the dark, I sometimes think I'm missing something. I could be missing something small, like a toe, and I wouldn't know it. I wiggle my toes and try to feel them all, but I can't. Maybe I should get out of bed to count and make sure none are missing, but I'm too tired to count.

When I sleep, I'm not me anymore.

I dream about sleeping in the backseat of an old car. There are bread crumbs all around the car and on top of it, too, so that the animals will come.

Dad wakes me up in the morning. He's sitting on my bed and his face looks darker with his beard growing back.

It's late, he tells me, are you okay?

I nod.

It's almost lunchtime. You hungry? asks Dad.

Not really, I tell him.

Dad rubs his hands together. They make a dry sound.

We have those sandwiches that Leo made, says Dad.

I want to sleep more. I turn over onto my side and close my eyes.

Dad says, Come on, Sebby, it's time to get up. His big hand squeezes my shoulder.

Come on, he says, what's wrong with you?

Nothing, I tell him.

Dad lets me ride on his back, all the way downstairs to the kitchen. My sleeping bag is not under the table anymore and I wonder where it is.

Dad puts me down on one of the chairs and goes over to the refrigerator to take out the plateful of Leo's sandwiches. He brings it over and sits next to me. We both look at the plate.

I'm not hungry either, Dad says, but I think we should eat. You're growing, you have to eat. He picks up a sandwich and takes a bite, then nods his head to show me it tastes good.

I sit back on my chair, away from the table, and I watch Dad eat. The cat comes into the kitchen to see what we're doing.

Hello, I say to the cat and he rubs back and forth against my leg.

Can I give him some turkey? I ask.

Dad shrugs.

If you eat some first, he says.

I pick up a sandwich and look at it for a long time. Then I take a fast bite and swallow without chewing too much.

Good, Dad says, two more bites.

So I take two more. Then I drop a piece of turkey on the floor for the cat.

Can we name him? I ask.

I call him Cham, Dad says, short for Champagne.

I think Cham is a good name.

Is he going to stay with us? I ask.

Dad finishes chewing. He brushes off his hands on his pants.

I think so, says Dad.

Your friend, the boy, came this morning, Dad says.

Okay, I say.

I don't know if I want to see Jackson, but I want to tell him about the cat, Cham.

You slept for a long time, says Dad. He stands up to put the rest of the sandwiches back in the refrigerator.

I need to write a letter, I tell him.

Dad's standing with his head resting back against the refrigerator door. You're becoming rather prolific, he says.

I nod.

Dear Ms. Lambert,

Before I turned into me, I was a girl like Mother and I know all the things that she did.

Mother put crumbs of bread around the car and on top of the car, too. She slept in the backseat and it was cold, so she held on to the loaf of bread. The loaf was small because she used a lot of it for the animals. Mother hugged the loaf close and she was warmer. When she woke up in the morning, all the crumbs of bread around the car and on top of the car were gone. The animals came in the middle of the night and I know how she felt. She felt like she missed something. I was feeling how she felt and it was a sad feeling.

Here is my hand. I can trace it really well now.

Bye, Sebby

I want to ride the yellow bike. I don't care about before. I've been thinking about riding and I know how to do it now.

I find the bike in the grass, in the place where I fell. I pick it up and I have to get on fast or it won't work and I'll tip over. I'm standing next to the bike and I do it. I get on and pedal as fast as I can. Then I have to turn or I'll crash into the house. It's hard to turn because it feels like tipping over, but I have to, so I make the bike turn and after, I stop slow and put my feet down.

I try again and I'm going. I know how to do it now.

Then I see Jackson and I fall. He's standing by the back door. He waves at me, but I don't wave back.

I'm okay. There's no blood in my mouth. I get up fast because I don't want the grass smell to stick on me.

What're you doing? I ask. I leave the yellow bike and walk over to him.

I got in trouble because of Halloween, he tells me. I can't have any of my candy for two weeks.

How did you get back here? I ask. I know he had to walk through the whole house to come out the back door.

The front wasn't locked, he says.

Dad forgets to lock the door sometimes, so I have to remember.

I have a cat, you know, I tell him.

Jackson's looking down at his red boots. He squats and rubs away a scuff mark with two fingers.

Let me see it, Jackson says.

I take him inside the house and we go to the kitchen but the cat's not under the table, so I go upstairs to ask Dad and Jackson follows.

Dad's lying on his back on the floor with his arms folded under his head. The cat's sleeping on Dad's stomach. I know the song playing. Dad has it turned down low because he's listening to the Beach Boys. I go sit by him and pet the cat. I look at Jackson to see how he watches me. He watches with his arms crossed, wrapped tight around him like a hug. I listen to the song. It's about the sun staying in your body and keeping you warm at night.

When the song's over, Dad looks at me and then at Jackson.

What're you boys up to? Dad asks.

Nothing, says Jackson.

I keep petting the cat. He's stretched out long on Dad's stomach.

You can pet him too, I say to Jackson.

Jackson shakes his head no. I have stick bugs, he says.

Oh, I say.

Jackson unwraps his arms. With one hand, he pulls on his bottom lip. He keeps pulling it out and then letting it go.

Do you want to see them? he asks.

Yes, I say.

Then Jackson runs back downstairs. Come on! he yells at me.

I gotta go, I tell Dad.

All right, Dad says.

Bye, I say and run down after Jackson.

He's outside already, waiting for me on the sidewalk. He starts walking when I get close, so I have to run again to catch up with him.

I keep them in a jar, Jackson says, they like to eat blackberry leaves. They're Shelly's too, he says, but mostly mine.

We don't talk for the rest of the way. I've never been inside of his house before and I wonder what it looks like. In my head, the inside is all blue like the outside, but I know it won't be like that really.

Jackson starts running then and I don't want to run, but I do anyway. He runs right into his house, so I do too, and we go all the way up the stairs to a big room that's got toys all over the floor.

I sit down next to Jackson and we look at the stick bugs in their jar. They're hard to find.

See, Jackson says, and he grabs a spray bottle. This is how you give them water.

He sprays two sprays in their jar.

They drink up the drops, he says, but you have to be careful when you spray, because if you squirt the water right on them, they'll get sick and then they'll die. Jackson licks his lips and he looks at me.

You can't spray, he says, because you don't know how to do it right.

I don't care about spraying.

The room where we are has brown wood on the floor and walls that are light yellow and over in the corner, there's a pillow fort with the plastic mat from Twister for a roof.

Is this your room? I ask Jackson and he looks around like he's looking for something.

There's no bed in here, stupid, he says, it's the playroom.

Shelly comes in then pushing a small baby stroller that has three Barbie dolls sitting in the baby seat. She stares at me but doesn't say anything and then she pushes her Barbie dolls over to the fort.

Shelly already killed one of the stick bugs, says Jackson.

You are a liar, Jackson Josiah, she says and runs out of the playroom, pushing her stroller with her. The wheels are loud on the wood floor.

It died on its back on the bottom of the jar, Jackson tells me. We had five and now we only have four.

I don't think it was Shelly who made the stick bug die. I can hear her pushing the stroller back to the playroom. She comes in with their mom.

The baby's sleeping, their mom says, and I'm going to be very upset if you wake him up. Their mom has red hair that's darker than Shelly's and I look at her feet because she doesn't have any shoes or socks on and her toenails are painted pink.

I didn't do anything, Jackson says. He's not looking at his mom or Shelly. He's looking at the stick bugs.

Hello, their mom says to me and I put up my hand to wave. She picks up one foot and leans against the wall. The pink on her toenails is pale, like the inside of seashells.

Shelly pushes her stroller over to where Jackson and I are.

You're a liar and an idiot, too, she says to Jackson.

He still doesn't look at her and doesn't say anything.

Shelly, please, their mom says. She stands there and watches us for a little bit. Then she goes away.

What's your mother's name? I ask.

Alison, says Jackson.

Shelly pushes her stroller so that it runs into Jackson's back.

Dad's name is Rockney and the baby's name is Baby Chester, Shelly says.

Shut up, says Jackson. He turns around and shoves her stroller backward.

Hey, Shelly says, but she goes away then. She pushes her stroller over to the corner with the fort.

That's my fort, says Jackson.

Shelly doesn't say anything. She takes her three Barbie dolls out of the stroller and goes into the fort with them.

Are you a Democrat or a Republican? Jackson asks me. His face is serious.

I don't know, I tell him.

Do you like Bill Clinton or not? Jackson asks.

I know that Cass's bumper stickers have the words CLINTON GORE.

I do like him, I say.

Then you're a Democrat like me, Jackson says.

I'm a Democrat, too! Shelly yells from the fort.

At the end of the pier, Mother dropped her favorite thing. It
was an owl that she carved out of pink soap. She dropped the
pink owl in the water to see if she would jump in to save it
and she did.

The owl was different afterward because it was soap, so
the water made it smaller.

First, I have to find my favorite thing.

EVIDENCE

In the closet, I find the box that says LOUISE AND ALEXANDER. I want to see a picture of Mother. I want to see her face. Most of the pictures are all the way down at the bottom of the box and there aren't people in them, just things, like a beach or some trees or food on a table. I keep looking. I open a yellow brown envelope and inside is a picture of Mother. She's holding a baby and laughing. You can see her face, but you can't see her eyes because they're closed. I slip it back into the envelope and then put that in my candy bag from Halloween.

I pick out two more things from the box. I choose a tiny umbrella—the kind they put in drinks at fancy restaurants. It's green and can open and close, but I only open and close it once, because I know it's old and maybe will break. The biggest thing in the box is a record. It doesn't have a case like all of Dad's records do. The record is black and yellow in the middle part and says, Steve Martin—Let's Get Small. I don't know who Steve Martin is. Maybe I will ask Dad.

I put the record in my candy bag and the tiny umbrella, too. Then I fold over the top of the bag so it's closed and slide it under my bed.

When I go back downstairs, the front door is open and Dad's outside on the porch steps. I go sit next to him.

Dad, I say, it's cold.

I'm working on my breathing, Dad says. The cold air helps. He takes a deep breath and then blows out all of his air until he coughs.

I put my hand on his back. You're okay? I ask.

I'm fine, says Dad.

I see then that he's not wearing any socks. His feet are long and skinny and the cold is making them purple blue. I touch his foot.

Dad says, I can't feel it—they're numb. He picks up one of his feet and shows me how the bottom is cut up and bloody.

I can't feel it, Dad says again.

What happened? I ask him.

I went for a walk, he says, I just wanted to walk.

Come inside? I ask.

He doesn't say anything.

Please, Dad, I say, and my voice sounds like I'm going to start crying, so Dad says okay.

We go in and I lock the door behind us. Then we just stand there together at the bottom of the stairs.

Dad says, Go get me a pair of socks.

I run upstairs and bring them back to him. Dad's sitting on the floor by the fireplace. He puts the white socks on his dirty, bloody feet.

We sit by the fire for a long, long time, not talking.

I want to say something, so I ask Dad, Who's Steve Martin?

Dad says, He's a comedian. You've seen him in movies. He's the guy from *Dirty Rotten Scoundrels*.

I found his record in Mom's box, I tell Dad.

Your Uncle Alex thought he was funny, Dad says. I can play it for you later.

Okay, I say. I want to know if Dad can feel his feet now and if they're hurting. I stare at his socks.

The cat is mute, Dad says. He doesn't meow or make any noises or anything.

But, I think he meowed at me once, I say, in the nighttime.

Really? asks Dad.

I nod.

You have to stay inside, I tell him. I keep looking at his feet.

Then I take off my glasses so everything turns blurry and the room looks softer.

Jackson tells me he will give me five dollars if I run all the way to the end of the pier that says DANGER NOT SAFE. I have a fat, black marker in my pocket. Jackson gave it to me so I can write something when I get to the end of the pier. The writing is for proof that I was there.

He's saying doll hairs, Shelly says. Listen to him.

I'm saying five doll-ars, says Jackson and he takes the five-dollar bill out of his pocket and holds it in front of us.

Where'd you get that? Shelly asks him.

Shelly's face looks different. I keep looking at her.

What? Shelly asks me.

He's looking at your funny face, says Jackson. He wipes his nose on his sleeve. She shaved off all her eyebrows with Mom's razor, Jackson says. She's a freak.

Shelly looks at me with her big moon face.

I like you, she says.

She's looking at me. I know I'm supposed to say something. Thank you, I tell her.

Jackson pushes Shelly back, away from me.

I'll count to ten, says Jackson, and then you go. Ready? he asks.

Count to twenty, I tell him.

Okay, Jackson says and starts counting. His voice sounds far away.

I'm looking all the way down to the end of the pier.

Jackson says, GO, so I go.

It's easy to run. It's like it's not me running. I can't hear my feet on the old, soft wood. At the end of the pier, I take the marker out of my pocket and write I WAS HERE. I look at my writing and I like how it looks. Then I run back. I'm running as fast as I can and in my head is just quiet. When I get to Jackson and Shelly, I fall down and lie there breathing.

The quiet in my head goes away and then I can hear Shelly.

You did it, she's saying.

Jackson sits down next to me and gives me the five dollars.

Here, take it, he says, what did you write?

I can hear my heart beating in my ears.

I tell him that I wrote, I WAS HERE.

Jackson's laughing at me, but I don't care. He keeps laughing and Shelly tells him to stop it right now.

You idiot, Jackson says to me, nobody knows who *I* is.

You stole that five dollars from Mom and I know it, says Shelly.

You don't know anything, Jackson tells her.

Shelly looks at me. Her face wants me to believe her and I do. I don't want the five dollars anymore. I sit up now and hand the money back to Jackson, but he won't take it. I try to drop it on his lap, but he jumps up fast and the five dollars lands on the grass. Jackson runs away.

Come on, Shelly says to me and she starts running, too. I don't want to sit there next to the five-dollar bill, so I run.

Jackson runs past his blue house and we follow him.

Slow down, Shelly yells, but Jackson won't slow down.

I run past her so I'm right behind Jackson now. We're running far, far away from the five-dollar bill. Jackson is running the way you go to get to the post office. I know this way.

You guys, Shelly yells from behind us, but we won't stop.

It's easy to run now. We go all the way to the park.

Jackson climbs up the clown-head jungle gym and sits at the very top. I climb, too. You can tell the jungle gym used to be painted blue, but now a lot of the paint is chipped off and it's just metal color.

There are two kids on the swings. They don't say anything to us. I watch them. They're pumping hard with their feet and swinging high. The swing chains make a moaning sound, like they might break.

Shelly's coming now. She's walking, not running.

I knew you'd run here! Shelly yells at Jackson.

He doesn't say anything.

The kids on the swings are a boy and a girl and they have white blond hair. The girl sticks out her tongue at us and I don't like how she stares. My stomach feels tight inside and I have to pee, but there's nowhere to go!

Shelly climbs up the jungle gym and tells Jackson to move. She pulls on his leg because she wants a turn to sit on the top, but Jackson shakes his head no.

Slowly, very slowly, Jackson pulls his feet up so that he's squatting on the clown's hat, and then with his arms straight out, he stands. The boy and girl on the swings are pumping and looking at Jackson.

Shelly pinches me on the back of my arm. I turn around and look at her.

Don't, I tell her.

Hey, says the girl on the swing. She kicks off one of her shoes and it flies at Jackson but doesn't hit him. Then the boy on the swings yells at us.

Get the HELL out of here! he screams. He has almost the same face as the girl. He kicks off one of his shoes and it flies way up high over our heads.

Let's go, Shelly whispers to me.

I want to run, but I hold on tight to the jungle gym.

Come on, Shelly whispers.

Shhhh, I tell her. I look up at Jackson.

He's staring at the boy and girl on the swings.

Screw you guys, Jackson says. He doesn't say it very loud.

Then he jumps up and twists around in a whole circle so he lands facing the same way. Shelly claps for him.

Good, Jackson, good, she says.

I know something bad is going to happen now. The girl on the swings kicks off her other shoe and it misses Jackson again.

Damn it, says Jackson. He squats low on the clown's hat.

Then I see the blood. His nose is bleeding down his face and dripping onto his shirt.

Jump down and run, Jackson says in a low voice. Try to get their shoes, he says to me. Shelly, just run, he says. Okay, ready, GO! Jackson tells us and we go.

I land hard on the ground and fall forward. My hands feel like they're burning. The boy and girl jump off the swings to get us.

Chickenshits! the girl screams.

I grab a dirty white sneaker and run.

You asshole! the boy yells. Give me back my shoe, you dick! You four-eyed dick! he yells. Does your dick have four eyes too?! You bunch of assholes!

I'm running as fast as I can and it's not easy now. It feels like tripping, like I'm going to fall. I have to keep going. Jackson's running next to me and Shelly's in front of us. I don't look back.

You assholes, the boy and girl are saying, we're going to beat the living shit out of you!

I can hear their voices behind us. Jackson's in front of me now. His blood is dripping and making spots on the sidewalk.

Come on! Jackson yells.

I can't go any faster. I have to pee really bad now and it hurts to run.

Follow me, he says and passes in front of Shelly.

Keep running, I'm saying in my head, keep running.

We go across a street and through a gate into the back-yard of a brown house and then we have to climb over a fence to get out. It's a brown wooden fence and there's a hole in the wood where you can put your foot to climb up. I have to throw the dirty shoe over first and then I put my foot in the hole and climb. It hurts my hands to hold on to the top of the fence and I slip going over so my leg scratches on the wood. The scratch feels hot on my leg and burns like my hands. I pick up the shoe and run.

We're running behind the houses, following Jackson. He opens a white gate into another backyard. After Shelly and I are in, he slams the gate shut.

We lost them, he says and breathes hard. There's blood all

down the front of his shirt and he's pinching his nose to make the bleeding stop.

You're dying, Shelly says to him.

Jackson lets himself fall down on the grass. We lie there in the backyard of a tall white house and catch our breaths. My hands are burning and the scratch on my leg is burning, too. I still have the shoe.

Holy shit, says Jackson.

I lift up my head to look at him. He's lying on his stomach.

Are you okay? I ask.

Shit, he says again.

Shelly sits up. Her face looks wet and splotchy red.

His nose bleeds when he gets nervous, she tells me.

You don't know anything, says Jackson.

I know about your nose, she says.

I sit up next to Shelly.

Close your eyes, I tell her.

Why? she asks. She pulls out a handful of grass and looks at me.

I look away. Please, I say.

Shelly drops the grass and then pulls up another handful.

You're really weird, she says and then closes her eyes.

I go behind a tree where she can't see me anyway. My pee makes a loud sound on the grass. I can't help it.

You're peeing, she says.

Don't look, I say.

She's looking when I come back from behind the tree.

You peed, she says and starts laughing.

I sit down next to her.

She keeps laughing and Jackson's still lying on his stomach, not saying anything.

Jackson, look, I say. I hold up the stupid shoe for him to see.

He lifts up his head.

You stopped bleeding, says Shelly.

Yeah, Jackson says and puts his head back down.

We'll bury the shoe, he says, we can bury it here.

I sit with Shelly and we wait for Jackson to get up.

Let me see your glasses, says Shelly. She grabs them off my face and puts them on.

Hey, I tell her, don't.

Everything looks blobby, she says and takes them off, then hands them over to me.

I don't say anything. I want to go back to the white house now and be with Dad.

It's getting dark, says Shelly.

Jackson sits up then and looks around the yard. The blood on his face is dry and crusty.

We'll bury it over in the corner, he says and points.

We dig the hole with our hands.

I can't do it, Shelly says. She stops digging.

My hands are red and stinging from sharp pieces in the dirt.

Just put it in, says Jackson, and we'll cover it up.

I drop the shoe in and Jackson pats down the dirt on top.

Then we stand back and look. You can tell that something's there.

Dear Ms. Lambert,

Dad says that Mother burned all the pictures of her face. In Mother's box, I only found one picture of her. She's laughing with her eyes closed and she's holding a baby. Dad says that the baby is Cass. Mother's laughing and she's leaning forward with the baby in her lap and her dark brown hair is long and shining. Behind Mother is a window that's white with light. Dad says that Mother had to keep this picture because the baby in it is Cass and Mother couldn't burn a picture of Cass.

I'm there in the picture, too. I'm a part of Mother, floating where nobody can see me. I can hear Mother laughing. She's laughing at Dad, who's behind the camera. Dad's singing the funny song "Tiptoe Through the Tulips" in a high, shaky voice, because Mother likes him when he does that.

I know that the picture of Mother is my favorite thing.

Bye, Sebby

I can't find Dad. I told him to stay inside, but I can't find him anywhere. I'm looking in his room and in the kitchen and also the bathroom. Maybe Dad's lost in the house or maybe he went outside again. He's not answering me.

I keep calling, Dad, Dad, Dad. I think he could be gone.

Then I look under his bed and there he is all the way back against the wall with the cat.

Dad, I keep saying.

He's not answering me. He's petting the cat and won't look at me.

Bye, I tell him and run away, downstairs and out of the house. I slam the door shut behind me as hard as I can.

Outside, I hear a bird squawking.

Be quiet! I yell at the ugly bird noise.

I run all the way to the blue house and ring the doorbell. I ring it again and again because I don't want to wait.

Just a second, their mom's voice says and I listen to her steps coming closer. When she opens the door, she's holding Baby Chester. He looks at me and then turns away, like he doesn't want to see me.

Hi, Sebastian, their mom says.

I follow her into the house.

They're playing upstairs, she tells me, unless they killed each other. Then she puts Chester down and he can walk by himself. She holds his hand and he takes tiny, wobbly steps.

I watch them walking together.

It's good that you moved here, she tells me, there aren't many kids in the neighborhood and Jackson and Shelly have done a fine job of scaring away the few who are around.

I don't say anything.

You must be a brave boy, she says.

I nod.

Well, she tells me, you can go on up.

Okay, I say. I run upstairs to the playroom.

Jackson's sitting on the floor eating peanut butter out of the jar.

Hi, he says. He licks off the spoon and then puts it back in his mouth to suck on.

I look around. Everything is the same as before except the fort in the corner is caved in.

Where's Shelly? I ask him.

He takes the spoon out of his mouth and looks at it.

How should I know? he asks.

I'm in my room, Shelly's voice screams at us, and I'm not coming out!

I sit down next to Jackson and cross my legs like his.

So, says Jackson, what do you want to do?

I shrug. Nothing really, I tell him.

Here, he says and hands me the peanut butter jar. Just use your fingers.

The jar's almost empty, so I have to stick my whole hand in to get the peanut butter out from the bottom. I put all four of my fingers in my mouth to lick it off and that makes me choke a little, but I don't care. The peanut butter tastes good.

You want to watch TV or something? Jackson asks.

I'm sucking on my fingers.

Okay, I tell him.

Come on, he says, we have to go to my mom's room.

His mom's room is at the end of the hall. Jackson runs in and jumps up on the bed. It's a big bed with a puffy blanket that has blue and white stripes. The curtains on the windows have the same blue and white stripes. I climb up with the peanut butter jar and sit down at the bottom of the bed with Jackson.

You gotta take your shoes off, he says so I do. Jackson clicks on the TV and goes through the channels fast.

I like it in this room. It's all blue and white. The TV is on a short, white table and underneath is a blue circle rug. There's only one picture on the wall. The picture is of Jackson's mom standing on a beach with Jackson and Shelly. Shelly is small and naked and Jackson is small, too. He's holding on to his mom's leg. His mom's wearing a blue flower bathing suit and white sunglasses and she's smiling with her head tilted sideways.

Where's your dad? I ask.

I don't know, says Jackson. He's still clicking through the channels.

I scrape out the rest of the peanut butter with my hand.

You like this show? Jackson asks. It's *America's Funniest Home Videos*.

I don't care, I say. I just want to lie down on the puffy bed. I am tired all over. The inside of my body is tired.

You're in a bad mood, Jackson tells me.

Yes, I say and lick the rest of the peanut butter off my fingers. I think about how I left Dad alone.

Are you going to live for a long time? I ask Jackson.

I guess, he says. He's looking at the TV. In fifty years, people are going to live on the moon, he says. I'll probably die up there.

Shelly comes in and jumps up on the bed with us.

What're you guys doing? she asks.

We're watching TV, dummy, says Jackson.

Shelly hits him hard on the back and his back makes a hollow sound.

Don't touch me, Jackson says.

Jackson's going to drive Mom crazy, Shelly says to me. She slides down off the bed fast and runs out of the room.

Stay out! Jackson screams at her.

The peanut butter's gone, I tell Jackson. Do you have any milk?

Downstairs, he says.

I try to watch the TV. A girl swings her golf club and it hits her dad.

Right in the balls, says Jackson.

I close my eyes and listen to the TV laugh. Then I let myself fall back on the bed.

Will you go downstairs with me? I ask with my eyes still closed. I hear Jackson jump down off the bed.

Come on, he says.

I get up. All the way down the hall and down the stairs, I think about Dad hiding under his bed. I could go home and hide with him.

In the kitchen, Jackson's mom and Baby Chester are playing on the floor with blocks.

What's going on? she asks and tucks her hair back behind her ears.

He wants milk, says Jackson.

Sure, their mom says, you can show Sebastian where the cups are.

She's building a tower with the blocks. She puts a yellow block on top and then opens up her arms and says, Tadaaaaa.

Chester knocks over her tower. The blocks are loud all over the floor.

Boom, Chester says and laughs.

Jackson hands me an orange plastic cup. I hold it with two hands and he pours the milk for me.

That's enough, I say.

I take a sip and then watch him walk over to Chester. Their mom is picking up the blocks that are all over the floor. Jackson holds Chester's hands to help him stand up and then he lets go.

Look, he says, Chessie's standing by himself.

Be careful with him, their mom says.

The inside of my cup is shiny orange plastic and when I drink, I can see my face at the bottom.

Their mom is looking at me when I finish my milk.

How are you? she asks.

I like your white sunglasses, I tell her.

Yeah, she says, I don't know what ever happened to those. She smiles now. Her teeth are crooked in front, but they are nice, white teeth.

Mother had brown sunglasses at the beach. She was rubbing coconut sunscreen on my chest and down my arms. I liked the coconut smell.

I see two Sebbys, I told her and pointed to one dark lens and then the other.

Mother smiled and pushed her sunglasses up to the top of her head. Now there's only one of you, she said. She reached out and touched the tip of my nose.

I have to go see my dad now, I tell Jackson and his mom.

I know if I don't go home, then Dad will be all alone.

I don't want to tell anyone, but it's here inside of me. I know things that happened to Mother and what she saw.

I was sleeping, but I could see Mother running in the dark.

The car came around the corner with its lights shining. Mother closed her eyes and ran into the lights.

I go straight to Dad's room and look under the bed. He's still lying on his back with the cat. We look at each other and this time I don't say anything. I leave him again.

In my room, I take out my paper bag from Halloween and find the picture of Mother laughing with her eyes closed. I put the picture in a secret pocket inside of my jean jacket and I go.

Outside, I hear the sound of cold like the sound in a freezer when you open it up. The grass is frozen and crunches every time I step.

I find the bike leaning against the side of the house and push it by the handlebars out to the sidewalk. I have to get on fast and start pedaling and then it will be easy once I'm going.

So that I'm not thinking about getting on the bike, I try to think about something else. I think about my grandpa Chuck. I say his name in my head and it sounds funny. It's not real to have a name for someone you don't know.

I'm on the bike now and I just have to keep pedaling so I don't fall. I ride past the post office and past the restaurant with the sign that says Mitchell's and then I don't know any of the places, but I keep going. I have to be far away.

I ride until I see a pier that's painted white. I know this is where to stop. Now I have to be careful, because if I stop too fast then I will fall. Gently, I push backward on one pedal and the bike slows down, and then I drag my feet to make myself stop all the way.

I leave the bike and walk down the pier with the picture of Mother in my secret pocket. The white paint on the pier is peeling off and underneath the wood is old. I don't like how the peeling paint looks like fish scales flaking off. Too many fish scales. I want to stop and touch where the paint is peeling, but I don't. I know what to do.

At the end of the pier, I take the picture of Mother out of my pocket. I kiss Mother's forehead and look at her laughing face for a long time.

Then I drop the picture into the water and watch it float. I wait for it to start sinking. It's supposed to sink down the way Mother's pink soap bird sank down when she dropped it in the water, but the picture keeps floating. I lie on my stomach and reach down. I touch the water with just one finger to test how it feels. The cold feels like burning and growing, like it's making my finger stretch out bigger and bigger. Then with my whole hand, I push the picture of Mother under. I hold the picture down and look at Mother's face underwater. Her face flickers like a light, on and off. I pull my hand out and it feels heavy, like it's not mine. Mother's picture stays underwater.

I stand up with my hand hanging down heavy and I watch the picture underwater. I'm waiting for Mother's picture to make me jump. Then Mother's face flickers dark and I jump in to save her.

The water hurts. I can't feel the cold like I did when I put in just my finger, but now the water stings. I try to kick. It's hard to move my legs. My legs are too heavy or the water's too heavy. My clothes are sticking to me, pulling me down. I try to kick and swim, but my body aches like it's tired. I'm holding on to the picture and I'm trying to kick my legs. Water splashes on my glasses so I can't see.

I don't know how to get out. I'm reaching up with my hand, but my hand is so heavy. I have to reach way up to the pier. I'm trying to hold on to the picture. I can't feel it in my hand anymore.

There's a voice calling. I can hear a voice yelling and then the voice is right there close to me. I'm crying and choking. Water's coming in my mouth and I can't breathe. The water's hurting me all over. I can't feel the picture of Mother.

The voice pulls me out of the water and then I can see the voice is a man. He's holding me and running. My body hurts like it's still in the water. I feel like I'm growing, like my body's stretching out and out and my head is growing up into space. I think maybe I will float away. I'll float back up to the trees. Maybe that's where I'm supposed to be, with Mother and Sara Rose.

The man is asking me where I live and I want to tell him. I'm trying to tell him. The white house, I think in my head. The white house with the birds. I think of birds. I try to tell him and then my head fills up with light.

Dad's holding me. We're sitting next to the fireplace where it's warm. I'm wrapped up tight in an itchy, thick red blanket. The blanket's so tight I can't move. I can just wiggle my feet and sort of twist back and forth and that's okay. I don't want to move. I hold still and let my body be soft and heavy. My body feels tired, like it's sinking down. The same sinking feeling I felt in the water. I want to sleep.

Dad's singing to me in a low voice, the Mamas and Papas song about a gypsy and the dancing bear. Mother used to sing it to me. I close my eyes and think of the bear dancing with rainbow ribbons flying. The bear has big, soft feet the way Dad has big, soft hands.

Dad stops singing. He's rocking me and he says my name.

Sebby, he says.

I don't say anything.

Sebby, he says again, what happened?

On the phone, Cass says that she's coming to get me. Her voice sounds mad.

No, I tell her. I don't want to go with her. I want to stay here.

Sebby, Cass says, you don't have a choice—I'll be there tomorrow afternoon.

I don't say anything.

Give the phone to Dad, says Cass.

I run upstairs and lie down on the bed where I sleep. This is my room now and I want to stay. I pull the pillow over my head because I'm not talking to anyone and I'm not leaving this room. Cass is mad and I won't go with her.

I can hear Dad coming. When he sits, my bed sinks down. Dad doesn't say anything. I want to kick and scream, but I can feel my eyes burning hot like I'm going to cry. I bite hard on the inside of my mouth to make my eyes stop. I lift up the pillow.

Why did you call her? I ask.

Dad looks out the window.

You scared me, Dad says and then he lies down next to me. I'm so tired, he says, can we just rest?

The room's darker when I wake up. Dad's shirt has a wet spot on it from my mouth drooling. I wipe my mouth on his shoulder and then I hold still. Dad's sleeping and I want to be sleeping, too, but I can't.

I know where the old man and his dead bird are. I know where to look and I can see them. The old man is awake and so am I.

Dad, I say, I'm awake. Dad, I say again.

What's the matter? he asks. His voice is tired and crackly.

I'm awake, I tell him, I want to listen to the record now, the one from Mother's box.

Dad rolls over onto his side.

Now? he asks.

Right now, I tell him.

Give me a minute, he says and he rubs his face awake with his hands.

I jump down off the bed and find my paper bag where I left it. I pull out the record.

Here it is, I say to Dad, come on. I walk over to the door and flick on the light.

Christ, says Dad. He stands up and holds his head.

My head's spinning, he says.

That's okay, I tell him.

Dad laughs a half laugh, like a cough.

I'm coming, I'm coming, he says and he follows me down the hall to where all the music is. Dad lifts the plastic top off the record player.

The record makes scratchy, popping noises and then it starts.

Here we go, Dad says. He lies down on the floor with his hands tucked up behind his head. I sit next to him.

On the record, a man introduces Steve Martin and calls him *the master of comedy*. Then there's clapping and people shouting yay and whistling, and after that, music plays.

Dad says, Oh God, I forgot about the banjo.

Is that Steve Martin? I ask.

Dad nods his head yes.

Why's the banjo funny? I ask.

You wanted to listen to this, Dad says, it gets better, I think.

The people on the record are laughing at Steve Martin and I'm watching Dad. He smiles sometimes, but he's not laughing.

What's funny, Dad? I ask.

Listen, says Dad.

I listen to Steve Martin talk about being on drugs and feeling small. Dad's laughing now, so I laugh, too.

Your uncle used to laugh so hard he cried every time he heard this, says Dad.

It's funny? I say.

Yeah, Dad says.

What's his job? I ask. What's Steve Martin's job called?

Huh? Dad says.

He's the master of comedy? I ask.

Yeah, I guess so, Dad says and laughs. He's a stand-up comedian.

Oh, I say.

I listen to Steve Martin talking about eating dinner in a restaurant and someone asks him if it's okay to smoke. Steve Martin says, Sure, is it okay if I fart?

I get it, I tell Dad.

He laughs at me.

What? I ask.

He keeps laughing at me and that makes me laugh, too.

Then Steve Martin says he's mad at his mom, who is 102 years old, because she needs to borrow money for food.

Dad stands up and turns off the record.

I want to hear it, I tell him, but Dad shakes his head.

Come on, I say.

Dad says, NO. His voice is loud and sharp.

That's enough, Dad says, just stop asking. You don't know, he says. Then he walks away.

I look at the record still spinning, but I don't know how to make it play again. I only know how to work tape players and also the new CD player in Leo's room at home. I watch the record spinning until it stops.

It's night now and I don't know what to do because I'm not tired.

Gray light comes in from the window and I think maybe it's almost morning. I'm lying next to Dad's record player. The floor feels hard and cold, but before, when I fell asleep, it didn't. The floor is different now. I get up and find Dad. He's sleeping in his bed and that's a good place for him to be.

Downstairs, I put on my green puffy coat and walk outside. I try not to think about the people watching me. People are watching me because I did what Mother did. I jumped in the water. On the phone, Cass said that I have to be careful and do things the right way, or else people will think there's something wrong with me. She said I have to think about what I do before I do it and I have to wear my coat. I don't know who told her that I wasn't wearing my coat.

I walk to where there are blood spots from Jackson's bloody nose. I follow the dark red brown spots to the playground and then I climb up the jungle gym. I sit way up high on top of the clown's hat and I wait for it to be morning. I know that I lost Mother's picture when I was in the water and now she is gone. I don't want to think about it. I don't want to think about anything.

I climb down and walk slow to the blue house. If I walk slow, then maybe morning will come. In my head I count, so that way I'm not thinking.

I ring the doorbell. Then I have to wait again and I'm tired of waiting. It takes a long time before the door opens and Jackson's mom is standing there in a yellow fuzzy robe.

She says, Sebastian, is everything all right?

I nod. She looks at me with her forehead wrinkled up. She says, Sebastian, honey, it's six o'clock in the morning.

I try to think of something to say. I look down at her feet. She's not wearing socks and her toenails are still painted the light pink seashell color.

Well, come in, she says.

I follow her and I watch how she walks on her tiptoes. I like how she walks like that. In the kitchen, she sits down at the table so I sit next to her.

Hmmmm, she says. She's looking at me, her lips pressed together in a small, tight smile.

I say, I need to talk to Jackson.

He'll be up in a while, she says, and then she looks behind her like there is something there to see.

Do you want some milk or juice? she asks.

I nod.

Milk or juice? she says.

I don't really care which one. In my head, I'm trying to pick. Milk or juice, milk or juice, milk or juice, I'm thinking and the words sound funny to me. The words are just words and I don't know which one to pick.

Sebastian, she says. Her eyes are looking at me, trying to look at my eyes.

Juice, juice, juice, I say—only I say it too loud.

Sebastian, she says my name soft and quiet. She's leaning forward trying to make me look at her.

I'll get the juice, she says.

I listen to her pour it. Then she sets a green plastic cup down in front of me.

Thank you, I say.

I don't want any juice, but I drink a sip.

Why're you up so early? she asks.

My sister's coming to get me, I tell her, and I have to go home.

Jackson's mom is sitting with her hands on the table and she's looking at her hands now. Is she a good sister? she asks.

I shrug because I haven't ever thought about that before.

I hope my children learn to take care of each other, she says. I was an only child, and it was very lonely growing up. She stands and pushes her chair in. She stays like that behind her chair with her arms folded together.

You mind if I make some coffee? she asks and I shake my head no.

I look at my cup of juice. I pick it up and drink it all. Then, I say her name.

Alison, I say.

She turns around fast.

Yeah, she says. She's holding a red-and-white-checkered dish towel.

I look at the dish towel and I tell her.

I hid, I say, I didn't want to go to Mother's funeral.

Jackson's mom sits down with me.

I think that's okay, she says. She reaches out and puts her hand on the table, close to me, but not touching.

Even some grown-ups choose not to go to those, she says. Her fingernails are short and the pink polish is almost all chipped off.

Look, I tell her, I finished my juice.

Good, she says and her hand knocks on the table two times.

Can I go see if Jackson's awake now? I ask.

Sure, she says, he's sleeping in a tent in the playroom.

Upstairs, I push open the playroom door slowly and take quiet steps. The tent is a real tent for camping. I sit down and tap on the door. It's a light blue door that zippers open and the rest of the tent is a darker blue color.

Jackson, I say, but nothing happens. Jackson, I say again. It's the morning, I say. I sit in front of the tent, waiting. Jackson, I say louder, please wake up now.

The tent door zippers open a little bit and Jackson sticks his head out.

What do you want? he asks. His face looks red and sleepy.

My sister's coming today, I say, and she's taking me back home. I have to go with her.

Jackson zippers the door all the way open. Then he lies back down in his sleeping bag.

Come in, he says.

I scoot into the tent. Inside, the light is blue.

I don't want to go, I tell him.

Jackson stretches his arms up to the top of the tent and sits up again. He's wearing dinosaur pajamas. The dinosaurs are all different colors and they look happy, like nice dinosaurs, not like real dinosaurs.

It's because you jumped off the pier, Jackson says.

I don't want him to know about that. I look up at the top of the tent. I can feel blue light all over my face.

I saw blood spots from your nose on the sidewalk by the playground, I tell him.

So what? Jackson says.

They're your blood spots and everybody can see them, I tell him, but I know how to clean it. If we pour Coke on them, the blood spots will go away.

Jackson's sucking on his bottom lip.

How do you know? he asks.

My brother told me, I say.

Okay, Jackson says and crawls to the tent door. He has to push around me to get out. I sit by myself in the tent and stretch my hands up to the top. My fingers look bluish, like ghost fingers.

Come on, says Jackson. He puts his jeans on over his dinosaur pajama bottoms.

Let's go, he says and runs downstairs.

I follow him. In the kitchen, Jackson's mom is sitting at the table holding her cup of coffee with both hands.

We're going to the park to play, Jackson tells her.

It's cold, she says. You have to put another shirt on over that and wear your jacket.

Jackson just stands there.

Run upstairs and put on another shirt, she tells him, or you're not going out.

Jackson turns and walks out of the kitchen. I can hear his feet running up the stairs.

We'll miss you, Sebastian, Jackson's mom says. Behind her the clock on the microwave says 7:08.

It's 7:08, I tell her, it's morning now.

She looks back at the clock.

Yes it is, she says and then takes a sip of her coffee.

Jackson comes back with a blue turtleneck over his dinosaur shirt.

Okay? asks Jackson.

Get your coat, she says, and your boots are by the door.

Bye, I say to Jackson's mom.

You take care of yourself, she says. Then she gets up and hugs me tight against her.

I step backward when she lets go.

You take care of yourself, I tell her. I think maybe that is the right thing to say.

Outside, the sky is white and flat and there's no sun.

Where're we going to get Coke? asks Jackson.

We're standing on the sidewalk in front of his house. Jackson puts his hands in the pockets of his coat.

Maybe in my refrigerator, I say.

I follow Jackson to the white box house.

Wait, I say before he opens the door. You have to be quiet, I tell him, because my Dad's sleeping.

Jackson doesn't say anything. He opens the door and goes in. Gently, I close the door behind us so it makes only a tiny clicking noise.

Got it, Jackson says. He's already back with a Coke bottle

that's almost all the way full. I open the door for him and he runs out.

I let him get way ahead of me. I have to think. I know soon I won't be here anymore. I know that in my head, but when I try to think about it, I can't. So I don't feel sad or anything. And I know that I lost Mother. I look up at the white sky and it's like all the outside colors are gone. The colors of the houses and trees are there when I look, but they don't have as much color in them.

Come on! Jackson yells. He's waiting for me at the place where the blood spots start.

I run to him. I don't want to think anymore.

It doesn't really look like blood, says Jackson.

I know, I say, but it is. I touch one of the blood spots. It feels the same as the rest of the sidewalk.

What do we do? Jackson asks.

I pour out a little bit of Coke onto one of the blood spots. The Coke fizzes. We lie down to watch it up close.

Let me do it now, says Jackson.

I give him the bottle and then I count. There are seventeen blood spots.

I'm going to be a stand-up comedian, I tell Jackson.

What? he asks. He's pouring out Coke.

You know Steve Martin? I ask.

Jackson shrugs.

I'm going to be a master of comedy like Steve Martin, I tell him.

You mean, like, tell jokes? asks Jackson.

Yes, I say.

But you never tell jokes, he says.

Jackson laughs at me. I try to think of a joke, but I can't think of any.

I can learn, I tell him.

A car is coming and we both look because no other cars have gone by. It's Mother's old green car. I think maybe Cass won't see me if I lie down flat on the ground.

What're you doing? asks Jackson.

Shhhh, I tell him.

Cass stops the car right next to us. I hear the sound of her rolling down the window. I stay on the ground and close my eyes.

Sebastian, Cass says, what're you doing?

I close my eyes tighter. I listen to Cass open her door and there's the dong, dong, dong noise that the car makes when you open the door with it turned on.

Sebastian, says Cass. She's close to me now.

We're cleaning the blood spots, Jackson tells her.

What? Cass asks.

We're cleaning the blood spots with Coke, says Jackson.

Sebastian, Cass says. Her voice is right by my ear. She puts her hand on my back.

Sebby, she says, come on. Cass holds me under my arms and pulls me up. I don't want to look at her.

I told you to stop, Cass says, you can't be doing this weird shit.

I don't say anything.

Cleaning blood spots off the sidewalk is weird shit, she says. Sebastian, are you listening to me?

Bye, says Jackson.

I can hear his feet running away down the sidewalk. I don't move and I don't look at Cass. The car is still making the dong, dong, dong noise.

Come on, says Cass. She pushes me into the car.

Cass drives the rest of the way to the white house. When we're there, I get out fast and run inside.

Dad! I yell.

Sebby, Dad says.

I run into the kitchen and Dad's sitting at the table. On the floor by his feet, my blue and green bag is packed up full.

Hello, Dad, says Cass. She's in the kitchen now, too.

Dad stands up and walks over to where she is. He hugs her and then Cass puts her hands on his shoulders and pushes him back.

Do you know what he was doing? Cass asks. He was cleaning blood, she says. What do you think about that?

Dad doesn't say anything, so Cass talks to me.

Sebby, she says, do you even know who the president's going to be?

I shrug.

I want to write a letter, I say.

Clinton got elected, says Cass. It's possibly the most important political event since you were born, she says to me or Dad. I don't know who she's talking to.

My friends are Democrats like Clinton, I tell her.
Dad laughs a quick laugh through his nose.
What? he asks.
Shelly and Jackson, I say.
At least your friends give a shit about the world, says Cass.
I want to write a letter, I say again.
Not now, Cass says, we're leaving.

THE BACKSEAT

It takes a long time to get home.

I don't want to sit in front with Cass, so I'm sitting in the back. There's just the sound of the car and wind. My head feels soft inside from being tired. I lie down and that's a good feeling because my head touches one door and my feet reach all the way across to the other. I like to push my feet against the door and that makes my head push backward into the other side. It feels good and tight, like the car is squeezing me and holding me in. The ceiling of the car has tiny pinholes so small you can't count them all.

Cass turns on the news radio. She looks back at me for a second and then faces forward again.

Pay attention, she says, you should know what's going on in the world.

I try to listen, but the voices are just words in my head. I can't understand them.

The car stops and I open my eyes. I can see a gas station sign—an orange ball with number 76. Sinclair dinosaur gas stations are my favorite. Leo says that all of the dinosaurs' dead bodies give us oil for gas and that's why Sinclair has the picture of a brontosaurus. When I was little I asked Leo what sound they made and he said the brontosaurus sounded like a giraffe, so we went to the zoo and listened to the giraffes, but I couldn't hear anything. Leo said they were making a quiet noise that sounded like this: *minu-minu*. I know that sound is not for real.

Cass is outside putting gas in the car and she knocks on the backseat window by where my feet are. She waves at me.

I'm going to run into the store, she says.

I think about how dinosaurs are extinct. It's sad to think of the world getting too hot or too cold and all of the dinosaurs lying on the ground together, dying.

Cass comes back and drops a Charleston Chew candy bar on my chest.

You're welcome, she says.

I wake up in my bed at home.

Hello, I say to the dark. I reach over and turn on the light that's on the small table next to my bed. The lampshade makes a gray shadow on the wall.

My Charleston Chew and my glasses are on the table next to the light. Maybe Cass left them there for me.

I slide down off my bed and put on my glasses. I don't want to sleep anymore. I want to get up and look around. I sit on the white circle rug by my bed and open my Charleston Chew. I think it tastes like dried-out ice cream. I eat almost the whole thing.

Then I pull open the table's drawer. I know what's inside. My book that's called *What Do People Do All Day?* by Richard Scarry—it's not really about people but about animals who look like people and wear clothes like people do. It used to be the book I needed to read every night before I fell asleep. Folded inside the book is the yellow piece of paper Mother left for me with the words to the Mamas and Papas song. Also in the drawer, I find my favorite scratch-and-sniff fruit stickers with almost all of the smell scratched off. The purple grape sticker smells the best, but I won't scratch it anymore because then it will be all used up. In the very back of the drawer, I have Mother's lipstick that I took out of her purse. I can't open it or touch it since that would erase all of her that's still there.

My orange flashlight is under my bed. You have to twist the top part where the light comes out to make it turn on. I twist it on and point the light out of my room, into the hallway so I can walk down to the kitchen.

I shine my flashlight on the refrigerator. I need to check the magnets. We have six magnets that are different kinds of fruits. I count them all. The fruit is made out of rubbery plastic and I used to chew on them when nobody was looking, but I don't chew on them anymore. You can see the chew marks and Mother used to say, Who's trying to eat my magnets? She pretended not to know that it was me.

On the refrigerator is a picture of Dad lying on the couch in his pajama bottoms with no shirt on and he's reading the big, brown dictionary. There's also a picture of Cass sitting on a pumpkin in the pumpkin patch and she's trying to hold Leo on her lap, but he's slipping down. Leo is only a baby in the picture and he's looking up at the sky, because he doesn't know he's supposed to look at the camera. Then there's a picture of me. I'm a baby wearing a diaper and I'm sitting on the floor with Dad's white headphones on, listening to music.

Those are the three pictures on the refrigerator.

I look in the drawer of the kitchen desk for the cat book. The cat book has the addresses of all the people we know written in Mother's handwriting. It's called the cat book because every letter in the alphabet has a different cat picture. Mother crossed out Uncle Alexander's name after he died, but she didn't cross out Grandpa Chuck's name and Grandmother's name.

In the downstairs bathroom, I lie on the floor so I can reach back into the cabinet under the sink and touch my piece of grape gum that I put there on my birthday when I was six. I have to feel around with my fingers and then I find it. It's hard now and mostly smooth, like a piece of plastic. I shine the flashlight inside so I can see. The gum isn't purple anymore, but darker, almost black.

Now I need to go to the room where Mother used to sleep with Dad. I shine my flashlight up the stairs and the wooden steps look yellow instead of brown. I walk slowly down the hall, past Cass's room.

On the floor of Mother's side of the closet, I open the box that has her red slippers. I don't touch them, I just look for a long time.

Then I open another box and find Mother's black winter boots. I reach inside and pull out the old note that says:

To Mother,
    Cass said you went out. Where did you go?
    I waited for you by the door. You took too long to come back, so I chewed the inside of my mouth. I know that is a bad habit to have. Are there good habits?
                            From, Sebby

I put the note back in Mother's black boot. I'm the only one who knows it's there.

Then I crawl over to Dad's side of the closet and reach all the way back to touch the cold handle of the secret door. It feels scary to touch the secret door in the middle of the night. I pull my hand away fast and jump back.

On Mother's side of the bed is a little table that looks the same as the one on Dad's side. I pull open the drawer to check for the book that Mother was reading. I know the book is called *Nightwood* by Djuna Barnes. But the book is gone.

I run into Leo's room. He's sleeping on his stomach with his covers kicked off onto the floor. I sit at the bottom of his bed and shine the flashlight on his pillow. I'm pointing the flashlight at his sleeping face, but it doesn't wake him up. His face looks very white and shiny, except for under his eyes are dark shadow spots.

I lie down on the floor in Leo's kicked-off covers. There's so much time in the night and I can't fall asleep. I don't want to be here in all of this time.

In the morning, I go downstairs and Cass is sitting with her feet tucked up on the soft, brown corduroy chair. The TV is on, but no sound is coming out of it.

Cass! I yell at her. I just woke up and I'm mad because she moved me back into my own bed.

Hang on, she says, I'm almost finished with this page. She's reading and not looking at me.

I want to see the name of Cass's book, but I can't because she's reading it behind her legs. I think she's sitting like that to hide the book from me.

On TV, it's The Snorks. Leo still likes to watch cartoons on Saturday mornings.

Where's Leo? I ask.

She doesn't answer.

I walk over and push the button to turn off the TV. I don't like to watch cartoons because there aren't any real people.

What? asks Cass and then she looks up at me.

Why'd you move me? I ask her.

Cass closes her book and tucks it next to her in the side of the chair.

I thought you'd sleep better in your bed, she says.

Don't move me, I say.

Cass wraps her arms around her legs and rests her chin on her knees.

What's wrong? she asks.

I don't say anything.

Leo went to the library, she says, he'll be back soon.

I sit down on the new couch and look at the empty, gray TV. I think about how the new couch isn't new anymore. We used to have a brown corduroy couch that matched the brown corduroy chair. Then Mother got sick of it and she pulled it out onto the front lawn. Mother hurt her back trying to move the couch by herself.

I sat with Mother. It was funny to be sitting on a couch outside, in the middle of the grass. We played UNO and then the sun went down and we couldn't see the cards anymore so we just sat. I got mosquito bites all over and Mother held my hands so I wouldn't itch. When we went inside, Mother put pink calamine lotion on my bites. She blew on each bite to make the lotion dry and that felt cold and good. Then she blew in my ear to tickle me and I got shivery. The next morning, a truck came to take away the old couch. Mother watched and cried.

I hate being here and I hate the new couch so I throw all the pillows on the ground and then I stand up and kick the couch hard. The kick hurts my toes. I have to sit down on the floor and squeeze my toes tight to make them stop hurting, but they hurt so bad, my eyes burn. I don't want to cry.

It's an ugly couch! I scream at Cass.

She gets up from the brown chair.

It's not my fault, Sebby, she says. She tries to pick me up, but I lean forward and make myself heavy so she can't move me.

I'm crying now and Cass lets go. She sits next to me on the floor.

Calm down, Cass says, please.

Where's Mother's book? I ask her.

What? asks Cass.

Mother's book that's called *Nightwood,* I say. It's not in the drawer. My voice sounds like I have a cold, because I'm crying.

Oh, Cass says, I'm just borrowing it, Sebby, I promise that I'll put it back.

But where is it? I ask her again.

Cass puts her hand on my shoulder. I push her hand away.

It's up in my room, says Cass.

No, I tell her. I'm crying and it's hard to talk.

You weren't supposed to touch everything, I say. I take off my glasses and throw them at her.

I don't understand you, Cass says. Sebby, please.

I lie down on the floor and cry. I don't want to be here and have to look around for everything to be right. Nothing's right. Time keeps making things happen. I lost the picture of Mother and now she's gone.

Leo will be home soon, Cass says, he just went to return a book.

I'm crying with my face in the dark under the ugly, new couch.

Cass isn't talking to me anymore and then her voice comes back.

Here, she says, drink some water. Will you sit up, please? If you drink this, says Cass, you'll feel better.

The ice makes cold, cracking noises. I listen to Cass set the glass down on the table. I don't want any water. I want to stay where I am on the floor.

Then I can hear the car driving up, crunching and popping over the gravel. Leo is home.

When he comes inside, Cass says, I don't know what happened.

Leo sits down next to me and rolls me toward him. His face looks scared.

I let him hold me.

We'll go for a drive, Leo says to Cass. He carries me out to the car and puts me in the backseat.

Cass's voice says, I'm sorry, Sebby. Then the backseat door pops closed. I'm by myself. I hold my breath to try to stop crying now. It's quiet inside the car. I like being by myself.

I remember when I got sick. My fever was so hot, Mother put me in the bath in the middle of the night. The water was cool. Mother dipped the washcloth in and then held it over my head so the water dripped on my face. I remember I was there, but also I wasn't there. It was hot inside my head and I couldn't think. Mother was talking to me and I was trying to listen, but I couldn't. I could hear her voice and I knew she was with me so I didn't try to listen anymore, and when I closed my eyes I was falling and falling backward. I could hear Mother's voice and I could feel her holding me, but I wasn't there.

Maybe that is what it's like to die. I don't want to live for a long time, because I lost Mother and now I have to find her.

Leo drives and doesn't say anything.

I wait a long time and then I tell him, I want to go back to Dad.

Leo's quiet.

Then he says, Okay, we'll see, maybe in a few days.

Do you like pigeons and all kinds of birds? I ask.

Yeah, Leo says, the birds are descendants of the dinosaurs.

What? I ask.

Birds are like the dinosaurs' children, he says. I watch the side of his face talking. Yellow morning light shines all around him.

Oh, I say, we can go home now.

Leo finds a movie to watch on TV. It's an old, black-and-white movie with cowboys. I'm on the floor because I don't want to be on the new couch. Cass brought me a pillow from upstairs to sit on. She's not mad.

I don't like the movie. The cowboys in it are real people, but they're not like how people really are. I ask Leo if there are still cowboys today.

Sort of, he says.

The doorbell rings and Cass and Leo look at each other.

Mrs. Franklin again, Cass says to him, you get it this time.

Fine, says Leo. He goes over to answer the door.

Mrs. Franklin, our neighbor, gives Leo a hug and comes inside. I made you an apple cobbler, she says.

Wow, thanks, Leo says and takes the brown grocery bag.

My goodness, says Mrs. Franklin when she sees me. How's my handsome little boy? She's smiling and blinking her big eyes.

We're watching a cowboy movie, I tell her.

She bends over close and says, You'll have to come and bake cookies with me.

I don't say anything.

Sebby would love that, says Cass, how about I'll give you a call?

Then Cass gets up and walks Mrs. Franklin to the door. Leo's telling her thank you again for the cobbler. He gives Mrs. Franklin another hug and then she leaves.

Leo looks at his watch. Less than five minutes, he says, I think that's a record.

Cass laughs and takes the bag with the cobbler into the kitchen.

What's a cobbler? I ask.

Like a pie! Cass shouts from the other room.

Or a person who fixes shoes, Leo says.

Cass comes back over and sits down on the couch.

What'd I miss? she asks.

I don't know because I haven't been watching.

I close my eyes and think about Dad in the white house by himself. I don't know if he is okay or not. In my head, I see him sleeping in the kitchen chair with his head resting on the table and that is good. I hope Dad is sleeping.

I ask Cass, Can we call Dad now?

Later, she says, we'll call him after dinner.

To make the time go by, I try to fall asleep.

In the dream, I'm in a square pen made out of wire with so many tiny baby chicks. The baby chicks are soft white and soft yellow. It's hard to move. If I move, I could step on a baby chick because they're everywhere and it makes me dizzy how there are so many of them. Someone is laughing at me.

Sebastian, says Cass's voice. I can hear Cass's voice saying my name and then I am me again. Cass is shaking me awake.

Sebby, her voice says and I open my eyes. Her face is close to mine.

I have a sick feeling in my stomach.

You were crying, Cass says and she wipes my cheeks.

I don't want to tell Cass my dream.

I'm sorry about before, says Cass. She stands up and holds out her hands.

I reach for her and then she pulls me up and I'm standing. I feel dizzy. I go into the bathroom and lock the door. The dream made me sick. I sit down in front of the toilet and I think I'm going to throw up. I rest my forehead on the cold seat and that feels better.

Are you all right? Cass's voice asks and she knocks on the door.

Yes, I tell her and try to make my voice sound happy. I move my forehead over to a new cold spot on the toilet seat. I stay like that for a long time and think about Mother. For her tenth birthday, Grandpa Chuck gave her too many baby chicks. She told me how they scared her.

Cass's voice comes back again.

Sebby, she says, please come out.

I'm tired and I don't want anything else to happen to me. I want to be with Mother. I lift my head up off the toilet and walk over to open the door. Cass is standing right there.

You're okay? she asks.

I nod.

I follow her into the kitchen and we sit down at the table.

Leo went out to get Kentucky Fried Chicken, says Cass.

I don't know if I'm hungry or not.

We thought you'd want mashed potatoes and coleslaw, she says.

I put my forehead down to rest on the table. It doesn't feel cold the way the toilet seat felt. I close my eyes.

Listen, Sebby, Cass says, tomorrow I'm taking you to the dentist and Leo will take you to get your haircut.

Fine, I say with my eyes still closed.

If you want to have Katya over that would be fun, says Cass.

I don't want to think anymore.

I don't know if she's my friend, I tell her.

Cass is quiet and I'm glad, but then she starts talking again.

Do you want to see your teacher? Cass asks.

No, I say, I'm not going back to school.

Cass says, Sebby, you know, you'll have to go back at some point.

Not now, I tell her.

Thanksgiving is Thursday, Cass says. The three of us can drive to the summerhouse, and if Dad is all right, you can stay with him.

Yes, I say. I think maybe Cass doesn't have anything else to tell me and I can rest.

There's a social worker, Cass says. Her name is Mrs. Alden. She's going to want to come check on you and Dad.

Why? I ask.

To make sure Dad's taking good care of you, says Cass.

He is, I tell her.

Cass nods.

I hear her scoot back from the table and get up. She walks away and her feet make noises like they're sticking to the floor. I know that's the sound feet make without any socks on.

Mother didn't like that sound. She always wore her red slippers and her feet swish-swished.

Cass turns on music. It's the song I like with the man singing about a blister in the sun.

Dance with me, says Cass. She's dancing with her hands up high over her head. She looks funny, but I don't smile.

I shake my head no. I don't want to dance. I don't like to.

Then Cass says, Please, please. She gets down on her knees and puts her hands together like she's praying.

I don't want to smile, but I do. Cass grabs my hands and pulls me up. She holds my hands tight and moves me around to make me dance.

I sing with Cass. The song gets quiet, like a whisper.

Here it comes, she says.

I know the song's going to get loud again.

It gives me the goose bumps, she says close to my ear.

It makes me feel like I have to pee, I tell her.

Cass laughs. We sing the loud part together as loud as we can.

When Leo comes in and sets the two bags of food on the table, Cass tells him to dance. He does the funny dance like he's swimming, going down underwater with one finger pointing up at the ceiling. Cass and I do it, too.

Then the song's over and Cass turns off the music.

So what's better, Leo asks, a song that goes quiet and then gets loud or a song that has a fake ending and then starts up again?

The food smells good and makes me hungry.

Why does it matter? Cass says.

Leo puts his hands in his pockets.

Well, he says, because they're two different things.

Cass shakes her head. She sets out the place mats and tells Leo to get plates.

We all sit down. There are six chairs at the table, so now we have three extra.

This food is so greasy, says Cass. She wipes her hands on one of the napkins and pushes her plate away.

Did you see the new clothes I got you? she asks me.

No, I tell her.

I left the bag up in your room, Cass says. I'll get it. She goes and I can hear her feet running up the stairs.

Ants in her pants, Leo says. He makes a funny face and wiggles around. I laugh.

Cass comes back with a white shopping bag. She pulls out a sweater and holds it up to show me. It's green with light blue and brown stripes.

You like it? she asks.

I nod.

She takes out another sweater. This one is light blue with a white polar bear on it.

Polar bears are vicious, Leo tells us.

Great, says Cass. She looks at Leo and rolls her eyes.

Then she shows me the pants. New jeans and new pairs of brown and blue pants.

Shoes, too, Cass says and pulls out a pair of dark gray sneakers. I didn't want to get white, she says, because they look dorky when they're clean and you're so careful.

Can I see? I ask her.

She hands me the shoes. The bottoms have a wavy line pattern with a big circle dot on the heel and smaller circle dots like toe prints. I trace over the lines and the circles with my finger.

They're good, I tell Cass.

I have something for you, too, Leo says, hang on. He stands up and, wiping his greasy hands on his pants, he goes.

Cass starts to clean the table. She crinkles up the bag that the food came in and throws it away, then takes our plates over to the sink and turns on the water.

Sebby, she says, is there anything else you need?

I don't know, I tell her.

Okay, she says. Cass just stands there with the water running. I want to run over and shut it off.

Leo comes back and hands me a thick book.

It's the *Guinness Book,* says Leo. It has all kinds of facts about anything you want to know about.

Thanks, I tell him.

The book is heavy on my lap. The cover says, *1985 Guinness Book of World Records.* There's a picture of a giant watermelon next to a laughing baby and a picture of E.T. and also, a picture of fancy shoes with jewels. Leo points to the shoes.

Each one is worth twenty-six thousand dollars, he says. Then he points to the watermelon. It weighs two hundred fifty-five pounds, he tells me.

Leo memorized the whole book, Cass says and she laughs.

I think about the whole heavy book inside of Leo's head and

then I think about 1985. In 1985 I was only one and Mother was still going to be alive for a long time.

I'll read it all, I tell Leo. I rub my hand over the smooth, hard cover.

You don't have to, says Leo. He's sitting with his elbow up on the table, holding his chin in his hand.

Can we call Dad now? I ask.

Cass nods. She gets up and dials the number on the phone. The dialing sounds like a song.

Cass says, Hi Dad, it's me. Sebby's been wanting to talk to you. She hands me the phone.

I tell him that I'm coming back.

I'll be there on Thursday, I say, and on Thursday it's going to be Thanksgiving.

Dear Ms. Lambert,

Dad is alone in the white house and Mother is dead with the baby, Sara Rose. I want to be with Dad and also with Mother, but they're never going to be together in the same place anymore.

I am here at home.

Cass says soon I have to go back to school. I don't want to yet. Sorry.

I do like you and I like how your black and white chapstick smells.

Bye, Sebby

From my bag of new clothes, I pick out blue pants and the polar bear sweater to wear. They smell kind of spicy clean from hanging up in the store and not being washed yet. I get dressed and then look in the mirror. I like how I look.

Katya is coming. I do want to see her, but it's strange how she doesn't know about the white house or Jackson or all the things I can remember. I don't want her to know.

I'm looking at my eyes in the mirror. I think about Katya's eyes. Hers are brown with yellow. I like Katya's eyes better than mine.

Sebby, Cass says.

I open my door. Cass is waiting for me in the hall.

Oh, she says, you look very nice.

Then she kisses my forehead and I wipe it off.

Katya is different.

Here, she says. She gives me a box wrapped in red and green Christmas wrapping paper.

Cass is standing behind me.

How nice, Cass says. Do you want Sebby to open it now?

Yes, please, says Katya. She's not wearing her yellow sweater or her green sweater either. She's wearing a pink sweatshirt that says GAP in big white letters.

Open it, Sebby, Katya says.

I peel off a piece of tape very slowly so I don't rip the wrapping paper.

Faster, says Katya.

I look at her. I can see the yellow in her eyes.

You do it, I say and hand her the box.

She rips off the paper and throws it on the floor.

There, she says and hands the box back to me.

I open the lid and look. It's a handkerchief.

Katya says, I sewed the *S* and Nana did the other sewings.

I look at the blue *S*.

Thank you, says Cass and she pinches my shoulder.

Thank you, I tell Katya.

What do you have in your room? Katya asks.

Go show her, Cass says, I'll be here if you need me.

Katya walks next to me all the way up the stairs and down the hall. In my room, I show her my box of Lincoln Logs.

I also have card games, I tell her, I have regular cards and UNO.

Katya sits down on the floor.

She says, Do you know that Mr. Martin and Mr. Lamowski are gay together?

I shake my head no. Mr. Martin was my second-grade teacher.

Katya says, I know your mother is dead.

I don't say anything. I can feel all the hairs on the back of my head and neck. It's a prickly feeling.

A lot of people are dead now, Katya says, that's what happens to people. Sit, she tells me.

I sit down on the floor with her. The carpet is light brown with pieces of dark brown mixed in. I run my hands back and forth over the scratchy carpet.

My grandpa is dead, Katya says. She pulls a piece of her long hair over to her mouth and sucks on the end of it. When she takes it out, her hair is wet and stuck together.

What do you do when you're not going to school? Katya asks. She pulls another piece of hair to her mouth and sucks on the end.

I shrug.

If you want to love me, Katya says, we have to touch our tongues.

Now? I ask her.

Katya sticks out her tongue and leans forward to me. I stick out my tongue, too, and then our tongues touch.

You love me, says Katya.

Okay, I say.

Katya stands up. I look at her shoes. They're clean white shoes with pink laces.

You got new shoes, I tell her.

I know, Katya says.

I look up at her.

Do you know any jokes? I ask. I have to learn jokes so I can be a stand-up comedian.

I don't think any of the jokes are funny, says Katya.

She's looking down at her shoes now.

Do you sometimes want to have a broken arm? she asks.

No, I tell her.

I know how to make you a cast that will look so real, Katya says.

I got new shoes, too, I say.

Katya looks at my feet and nods.

Come, she says, I will make a cast for you on your arm. We have to be in the bathroom for making the cast, Katya says.

She follows me to the upstairs bathroom.

Take off your sweater, says Katya.

I take off my sweater and look at myself in the mirror in my white T-shirt. I watch in the mirror how Katya touches my arm.

Okay, she says and pulls me over to the sink. She rips off pieces of toilet paper and puts them in a pile. Then, one at a time, she makes the pieces wet and wraps them around my arm. She covers my whole arm in wet pieces and then she puts dry pieces over the wet ones.

Do you look at your eyes in the mirror? I ask her.

No, she says.

Katya keeps working on my arm.

Now you hold it very still, she says, and it will be dry.

I look at my arm and try to hold it still. The cast looks a little bit real.

Sebby, Cass calls for me.

What?! I yell back at her.

She finds us then in the bathroom.

What're you guys up to in here? she asks.

Look, Katya says and I hold out my cast.

Wow, says Cass. She's smiling at Katya.

We can go for a walk now, Katya says, but he is too sick because of his broken arm, so I must push him in a wheelchair.

No, I say. I look at Cass.

It's cold outside, Cass says.

The cold is good for you to breathe, says Katya.

Well, we don't have a wheelchair, Cass says. Maybe we still have the red wagon in the garage.

Good, Katya says.

No, I say. I'm looking at Cass, but she won't look at me.

I don't want to go, I say.

Please, says Katya.

Cass crosses her arms. Be a good sport, she says to me, Katya is your friend.

Cass grabs my arm that's not in the fake cast and we walk downstairs. The garage is so full of old stuff, there's no room for a car.

Stay here, Cass says and lets go of my arm. She knows where to look for the wagon.

Katya stands next to me. The garage is cold and my teeth start to chatter. I look at our tree in the front yard. It's just sticks now.

Cass finds the wagon in the very back corner. Holding it up over her head, she carries it to me and Katya.

He's cold, Katya says.

Cass pulls down the old blue blanket that's folded on top of a box. She wraps it around me. The blanket smells old and dirty like the garage.

Get in, Katya says to me. She's holding the wagon handle.

Go ahead, says Cass.

I get in the wagon. Cass tucks the blanket under me and wraps it around me tight. Then Katya pulls me down the driveway. The wagon bumps over gravel and that makes the inside of my head buzz. I turn around and look at Cass. She waves.

Don't stay out too long, she says.

Then I hold up my hand that's not in the fake cast and I stick up my middle finger at Cass. I've never stuck up my middle finger at anyone before, but I know what it means and I mean it.

On the way to the white house, Cass and Leo take turns driving. I fall asleep across the backseat and then we're there.

Dad's music is playing too loud. Inside, I have to cover my ears and listen through my hands. The Beatles are singing about a hard day's night.

Leo and Cass follow me upstairs to where Dad's lying on the floor next to his speakers.

Cass turns down the music. What are you doing? Cass asks and Dad sits up.

I'm having a Beatles party, he says.

What? Leo asks.

A Beatles party, says Dad. I'm playing all the songs in order. Some songs I have to listen to more than once, he says, because they're too good.

In order of the American release or the UK release? Leo asks. He wipes his nose with the back of his hand.

American, Dad says.

Oh, Leo says and walks away.

It's Thanksgiving, Cass tells Dad.

I know, says Dad. He lies back down on the floor and folds his arms across his chest.

Shouldn't we make a turkey? Cass asks.

I'm not very hungry, Dad says, whatever you want.

Cass turns the music back up then. The Beatles are singing about how they should've known better.

Come on, says Cass. She grabs my wrist and pulls me downstairs to the kitchen. Leo's already sitting there at the table.

Do you want to have Thanksgiving or not? she asks Leo.

I don't care, he says.

Cass pulls me so that I'm standing in front of her.

Do you care? she asks me.

I shrug.

Let's just go then, Cass says. What's the point?

No, I say, and I run through the house, out the back door. I hide in the shed with the gasoline smell and nothing moving. I hold very still and wait.

We don't have to leave! Leo's voice shouts. Sebby where are you?

In here! I yell.

Leo finds me. Come on, he says, it's freezing.

CYPRESS AVENUE

In the morning, Dad's still having a Beatles party. I lie down on the floor next to him and listen to the song. It's about a girl who comes in through the bathroom window. I know all the words.

The volume is turned down low. Cass made him keep it that way for the night so we could sleep. I reach out and twist the knob. I like to make the music get louder and then softer again, because it sounds like the music is coming closer and then going away. Dad covers his ears. He hates when I do this.

Not now, Sebby, Dad says.

I stop playing with the volume.

What time is it? he asks.

I don't know what time it is now, but when I woke up, the clock in the kitchen said 6:37.

After six-thirty-seven, I tell Dad.

He rolls over onto his side and looks at me.

I've been listening for almost sixteen hours, says Dad. His breath smells bad.

I ask him where the cat is.

Probably under the bed, he says.

Cass is mad at you, I tell him.

Dad puts his heavy arm across my chest. He whispers to me, The party's almost over.

We listen to the song about going back home.

Cass is making soup and I'm helping. We found a red stool under the sink for me to stand on so I can chop the carrots.

Is he ever planning to come downstairs? asks Cass.

He's asleep, I tell her.

I'll wake him up for lunch, Leo says.

Leo's sitting at the kitchen table playing a card game by himself. Last night, he taught me how to play gin rummy and we waited a long time for Cass to come back from the grocery store. She drove all over looking for a turkey, but there weren't any left.

I have to use one of the regular knives to cut the carrots since Cass won't let me use the big knife. It's hard to cut with and I have to keep resting my hand.

We're making birthday soup, like Mother used to make on everyone's birthday, except we don't know what the secret ingredient is. Mother wouldn't tell us until we grew up and had our own kids. Today isn't anyone's birthday, but Cass said that doesn't matter.

What's your favorite Christmas song? Leo asks.

It's too early for Christmas songs, Cass says. She's stirring the soup with one hand and adding salt with the other.

It's just a question, says Leo.

"Little Drummer Boy," says Cass. You?

"O Holy Night," Leo says, just for the fall-on-your-knees part.

Yeah, you would like that one, Cass says.

Leo laughs.

I like the song that's about parsley, sage, rosemary, and thyme, I say.

That's not a Christmas song, says Leo.

I stop chopping the carrots.

But I like listening to it for Christmas, I tell him, it sounds right.

I agree, Cass says and smiles at me.

Dad comes into the kitchen then.

Birthday soup, he says, smells good.

Cass is staying here with us, I tell him.

Sebby, she says, you can't keep your mouth shut for five damn minutes.

Cass pushes on my shoulder and I have to step down off the stool so I don't fall.

Who's going to be with Leo? Dad asks. He sits down at the table.

Leo's shuffling his cards. Jesus, he says, I'm a big boy—I can take care of myself.

I get back up on the stool and keep cutting the carrots.

Want to play rummy? Leo asks.

Sure, says Dad.

It wouldn't even be a problem if we all stayed at home like normal people, Cass says. She takes the carrots from me and dumps them in the soup even though some of the pieces are too big.

I go over to the table and watch Dad and Leo playing cards.

We can deal you into the next round, Leo says.

I don't want to play, I say.

Dad lets me sit on his lap.

Do you know the secret ingredient? I ask him.

The secret ingredient is for growing and being happy and strong.

She never told me either, says Dad.

Leo wakes me up early to say good-bye. I follow him downstairs.

Dad's awake, standing by the door. You're sure you don't want to go out for breakfast first? Dad asks.

I have to get going, says Leo.

Dad and I watch him put on his coat and boots.

Well, Leo says.

I'll walk you out, says Dad.

Me too, I say.

Not dressed like that, Dad tells me.

So I put on my coat and new gray shoes. I can slip my feet in without even untying them.

Then I run out and Leo's sitting in the green car with it already running and the door open. Dad's using the scraper to get the ice off all the windows.

I wish you'd stay with Mrs. Franklin, Dad says.

I'll be fine, says Leo. He gets up and hugs Dad first, then me.

Be good, Leo tells me.

We watch until the green car is gone. I'm holding Dad's cold hand.

Leo gave me his *Guinness Book,* I say.

That was nice of him, says Dad.

We're walking back to the house and he's looking over his shoulder at the driveway where the green car was. I don't know what he's seeing.

You know, I say, there's a parrot named Prudle who knows a thousand words. That's the most words of any bird, I tell him.

He doesn't say anything.

Dad, I say, do you want to go out for breakfast?

I'm sitting by the fireplace, making a list. Yesterday Cass found a Polaroid camera in the closet, and my list is of all the things I want to take a picture of: 1) the cat, 2) the yellow bike, 3) the broken pier, 4) Dad's face.

The doorbell rings and I have to get it because Dad's in the shower and Cass is still sleeping on the cot we set up for her next to my bed.

I open the door just a little bit and see Jackson.

I'm making a list, I tell him.

Jackson's playing with the zipper on his coat, pulling it up and down.

Let me in, he says.

I open the door for him and then go back to the fireplace where my list is. Jackson comes and sits next to me. He takes off his coat and drops it on the floor by our feet.

My mom said to ask if you and your dad will come over for dinner, Jackson says.

I nod yes.

You have to tell your dad, says Jackson. He looks into the fire. We could burn something, he says. What's that? He points at my list.

My list, I tell him. I'm getting a camera.

You don't need it, he says. He grabs my list and throws it in the fire.

We watch the paper crumple up and burn into black.

I can remember the list in my head: 1) the cat, 2) the yellow bike, 3) the broken pier, 4) Dad's face.

Where's your dad? Jackson asks.

I tell him that Dad's in the shower. I listen then and the sound of running water is gone.

I guess he's out of the shower now, I say.

Do you want to go to the park? Jackson asks and picks up his coat off the floor.

No, I tell him, I'm going with my dad to buy film.

Jackson stands up and puts on his coat.

Fine, he says. He reaches into his pocket then and pulls out a white piece of folded-up paper.

Here, he says, it's from Shelly.

I take it.

See ya, says Jackson and he goes.

I open up the white paper. The picture is of the sky with a rainbow and a hot-air balloon. There are also two birds flying. One bird is red and the other is blue and wearing glasses like me. At the bottom of the picture it says, For: Sebastian, From: Shelly.

I fold it back up and put it in my pocket. In my head, I have the list of pictures I need to take and now I think of more: 5) the blue house, 6) Jackson's mom, Alison, 7) Dad's scar on his stomach.

I can hear Dad coming downstairs.

Sebby, he calls.

I'm here, I say.

Dad comes into the fireplace room. He's wearing his jeans now and a different T-shirt that's dark blue and says WELLESLEY in white letters. He sits down next to me. I lean in close to him and smell by his neck. Dad smells like the white soap.

I have to take lots of pictures, I tell him.

Yeah, Dad says, how many?

Seven, I tell him, but I'm still thinking.

The cat comes over to us. He rubs against Dad's legs and then jumps up by the fireplace where Dad put a pillow for him. I watch how the cat has to turn in circles before he lies down.

Jackson's mom wants us to come for dinner, I tell Dad.

He stops petting the cat.

What? he says. Why? We're fine. We don't need their dinner. He leans forward and holds his head. For Christ's sake, Dad says.

Cass is laughing and talking on the phone to Emma. She sees me watching her and says, Come say hi.

I shake my head no and run away upstairs. Dad's on the floor sleeping with his music playing. The song is one I know, about being eight miles high.

I sit down next to him and take a picture of his sleeping face. The square photo comes out of my camera and I have to shake it and wait for the colors to show up. On the white part at the bottom, I write, Dad's face, and then I look at my new watch that Dad bought me. It's black and Velcros onto my wrist. It says the time and the date so I also write, December 4, 1992, 7:14 PM.

I have to take a picture of Dad's scar, too. I lift up his T-shirt to see it. I know his scar will be there forever.

I take the picture and wait for the colors. On the bottom I write, Dad's scar, December 4, 1992, 7:15 PM. Then I put Dad's shirt back down over his stomach.

Now I've taken all the inside pictures.

I stand up and look at Dad sleeping on the floor. He looks small. His socks are stretched out funny and they're falling off his feet. I take a picture of his feet like that and then I write the time and the date.

In Dad's room, I find clean socks rolled up in a ball. I bring them back to where Dad is sleeping and I sit down by his feet.

It's easy to pull off his dirty socks. The new socks are tight and hard to pull on.

I crawl over to Dad's sleeping face. He can't see me, but I am here and I can see him.

Dad, I whisper, I need to be with Mother.

His arm has a little scab. I pick it off and a dot of red blood comes out of Dad's skin. Just a dot of blood.

I don't hear Cass coming, but there she is standing at the top of the stairs.

Sebby, she whispers, let him rest.

I go over to her. She takes my hand and we walk downstairs to the kitchen.

I made hot chocolate, she says.

We sit at the table and Cass tells me she's going to visit Emma for the night.

I'll leave her number right over by the phone, says Cass, in case you need to call me.

She gets up then and pours hot chocolate into two mugs.

Marshmallows? she asks.

Yes, I say.

She brings the mugs and a bowl of marshmallows to the table.

Will you sleep here tonight? I ask her.

I don't want her to go yet, because Dad already fell asleep and I like her being next to me in the cot by my bed.

How about I go after you're asleep, Cass says. I'll be back tomorrow.

Kiara Brinkman

I drop marshmallows into my hot chocolate and watch how they melt.

You could come with me, she says.

No, I tell her.

I try to take a sip, but the hot chocolate's too hot.

At night, when Mother was a girl, she walked in circles around the outside of her white house. She couldn't walk around inside because the floor made spooky creaking noises. So she waited in bed and watched the white numbers on her clock. When the clock said 11:30, then Mother got up and she walked in circles and circles. She didn't go away from the house where the dark was really dark. I know why. Because the dark far away from the house is different. It feels cold and empty. I know how it feels.

In her head, Mother made a decision. She didn't want to sleep anymore. Sleeping made the time go too fast.

To find Mother, I have to walk in circles and then she will take me with her.

It's snowing on me. I don't feel cold.

The snow is quiet. If I hold very still, I can't hear any sounds and then I have to make a noise so that I know I can still hear.

Circles and circles make the time go slow. There is too much time. I want to run to make the time go faster, but I'm so tired.

What happened? Dad's asking me. He keeps asking.

I don't remember. I don't remember going to the shed and falling asleep.

My feet and hands are in bowls of warm water. Dad's walking back and forth. He's walking and looking down at the floor.

You're very lucky, says Dad.

I can feel the bones inside my feet and hands, hurting. I have to keep them in the bowls of warm water.

You gotta stop this shit, Dad says.

I tell him okay. Don't tell Cass, I say, please.

Dad doesn't say anything.

Please, I say.

Dad sits down. Then he gets up again and walks back and forth. He stops and hits the table hard with his fist.

Dad, I say.

Dad's holding his fist.

He's screaming, Oh fuck, shit! He bends over and falls forward on his knees.

Dad's screaming, Fuck! His forehead is on the ground and his shoulders are shaking. He's crying. He's crying and saying, Oh fuck. His voice is lower now, like a whisper.

Dad, I say again, but he doesn't hear me.

Dad's sitting with me at the table. He's watching me write. I'm showing him that I can do it.

See, I say. My hands are working. I can use my hands. I can wiggle my toes, too. My hands and feet are not hurting anymore.

I'm writing,

Dear Katya,

I live in a white house that's very far away from you.

A cat lives here, too. He is my cat and also my dad's.

Remember, we were sitting on the brown carpet and you asked me what I do in the day instead of school. I'm taking pictures with my camera.

I have new friends. Their names are Jackson and Shelly.

You were not nice to me and I don't want to love you anymore.

From, Sebby

Dad says, Katya is your friend.

I shake my head no.

We're not sending the letter, says Dad, you have to be nice to people.

I put down my pencil and it rolls off the table. I watch it land on the floor and roll away until it stops.

She's not nice to me, I tell Dad.

That doesn't matter, he says. He goes and picks up the pencil with his good hand. His hurt hand is wrapped up in an old white T-shirt.

I don't say anything. Dad's looking out the window now so I look out, too. It's snowing outside. Pieces of snow stick to the window.

Then Dad starts saying the words to the song that Van Morrison sings. He says the words about girls rhyming on their way home from school. Dad talks like he's saying something mean. His voice is hard and he's looking out the window at the snow. He says the words about leaves falling and not being able to speak.

The words get stuck in Dad's head and then he has to let them out. This has happened before.

He's standing up with his arms crossed against his chest and his head rocking back and forth. He's saying the words faster and louder.

Dad says the words about cherry wine. His head is rocking and his hand bangs against his chest with each word.

Dad! I yell at him.

He stops then and looks at me.

I'm sorry, he says and he goes.

I follow him and watch him run fast up the stairs. Dad holds out his hand to tell me not to come.

Sebby, he says at the top of the stairs, leave me alone.

I stop and then the house gets quiet. I want Cass to come back from Emma's now.

I look at my new watch. It says 4:57 PM. I don't know what to do.

I walk outside. The sky is low and flat with no clouds. There's snow everywhere. In my head, a line connects the house where I live to the blue house where Jackson lives. I follow the line that goes straight, then right, then straight, then left—the line makes a shape like a hook.

The blue house is sad today. I stand by the mailbox, looking. The upstairs windows are white from pull-down shades. Nobody's home. In front of the door, a newspaper is waiting.

I reach out and put my hand on the cold, black mailbox. I leave my hand there until my hand is cold and I watch the house look sad. The roof is white from snow.

I put my cold hand in my pocket and then walk up to the blue house. What I do is just sit on the front steps. I know I can't stay for very long because I promised Cass I'd come back soon. She made me look at my watch. Thirty minutes, she said.

I take the letter out of my pocket. Dad gave it to me.

I can't, he said, I can't keep this anymore. He said, I'm sorry.

I unfold the letter again and look at it. I know all the words. The letter says,

Feb. 14, 1984

To my Sebastian,

Today, you are five days old. I have to tell you this now. When I hold you, I get a strange feeling inside. I feel like I am missing you even when I'm holding you, even when I'm looking at you right there in my arms. I don't know what this means. Maybe you will understand. Please, try to understand. You're sleeping right now. I watch you sleeping and I miss you. I need you to know how much I love you. I need you to know and hold on to my love always.

Yours, Mother

I look at the words. Then I fold the letter and put it back in my pocket, but I can still see all the words in my head. The words are just words from reading them too much and I don't know what they mean.

Snow is falling again, hiding the houses and the trees and the street. I run. If I stop, the snow will cover me up and make me disappear. I run the line that is like a hook all the way back to Dad and Cass.

Dad wakes me up late at night. I can hear Cass talking and laughing on the phone downstairs.

John Lennon died exactly twelve years ago, Dad says and carries me into his room. The TV whispers and flashes colors. I want to touch the warm screen.

Dad points to the black alarm clock next to his bed. The green numbers are blurry without my glasses on, but I can read them. The clock says 11:02 PM.

This is when it happened, Dad says, five shots.

On TV, there's John Lennon, not dead. He's saying, Everything we do is aimed at peace.

I hate these retrospectives, Dad tells me.

I watch a blurry picture of John and Yoko sitting together in a big, white bed. The picture changes to another picture of John and Yoko lying together on the floor and then the pictures flash faster and faster so you can hardly see them. The TV screen goes black for a second and there's a still picture of John Lennon's face with dates too small for me to read.

What's it say? I ask Dad.

Nineteen forty to nineteen eighty, says Dad.

I scoot down off the bed and touch my hand to John Lennon's warm face. It pops with static.

Come here, Dad says.

I lie down with my head on his leg and close my eyes. Dad puts his hand on my back.

Cass helps Dad get ready for dinner at Jackson's house. She straightens his collar and fixes his hair and gives him Tylenol to make his hurt hand feel better.

Try to be friendly, Cass says.

Before we go, Dad unwraps his white T-shirt bandage. He sees me looking at how his hand is dark purple blue and swelled up.

I'm fine, Dad says.

It's snowing again. The sky is sinking down low and turning dark for night. I'm walking, looking up. The dark is coming lower and closer. Snow lands on my face and stings when it melts.

At the blue house, I knock on the front door and I can feel Dad standing there behind me.

Jackson lets us in.

I have to take Dad's good hand and pull him inside.

Hi, Jackson says and then runs away.

Jackson's mom comes out from the kitchen. She's wearing a white sweater. I look down at her feet. Today she's wearing socks. Thick, white socks.

Hi, Sebastian, she says to me, how are you, honey?

I don't like your socks, I tell her.

Sebby, Dad says. He grabs my arm and squeezes too hard.

It's all right, she says. She's looking at her feet and then she looks up at Dad. We've never met, she says. I'm Alison.

Stephen, Dad tells her.

Shelly comes running out of the kitchen then and hides behind her mom.

This is Shelly, their mom says, and you've already met Jackson.

Dad nods.

We go sit down in the room with a tan-colored couch and chair. The TV's turned on and there's a JELL-O commercial with Bill Cosby's big, squishy face. Jackson's mom reaches for the remote on the table and clicks it off. In the empty screen, I can see Dad and me sitting next to each other on the couch. Dad crosses one of his legs on top of the other and shakes his foot.

Jackson! their mom turns and calls into the kitchen, come out here and bring your brother. She's sitting on the tan chair and Shelly's on the floor in front of her.

Hang on! Jackson yells back.

Their mom looks at me and Dad and says, I'm so glad you two could come.

Dad coughs and clears his throat.

You're Sebby's dad? Shelly asks.

Yes, he says to her, yes I am.

Shelly stares at Dad. I look at his face, too. His skin is very white and I can see that he's sweating. There are dots of sweat around his nose and above his lip and also on his neck.

P-p-p-pleease, says a funny voice from the kitchen. Jackson comes out then. He has on a plastic Roger Rabbit mask and Baby Chester's wearing a Jessica Rabbit mask. They're walking over to us, but slowly, because Baby Chester takes tiny steps.

Oh, Jackson, says their mom.

Baby Chester's a lady, Shelly says and she laughs.

Take those masks off now, their mom says.

Jackson pushes back his mask so that the plastic Roger Rabbit face is on top of his head and then he pulls off Baby Chester's. Shelly runs over to him and grabs the Jessica Rabbit mask. She puts it on and jumps up on the coffee table in front of the couch and starts dancing.

Okay, their mom says, that's enough. She stands up and takes off Shelly's mask.

Get down, she says to her.

Shelly sits on the table and looks at me and Dad.

Did you see the movie *Roger Rabbit*? she asks us.

I think so, Dad says.

I'm not allowed to, but Jackson saw the video of it at his friend's house, she says, and Jessica Rabbit has enormous boobies.

So, says their mom, these are my children—the lovely masks are courtesy of their father. She's holding Baby Chester on her hip. This is Chester, she says to Dad, my youngest. Then she sits down again.

I have three children too, says Dad.

I'm sure yours are better behaved than mine, she says.

Well, Dad says, they're older. He clears his throat and then doesn't say anything else.

I watch Dad's foot shaking.

Hey, says Jackson and he climbs over the back of the couch and sits down next to me.

Do you want to spend the night? he whispers. We can sleep in my tent.

Could I use your bathroom? Dad asks and stands up with his bad hand behind his back. He pushes back his hair with his other hand and I can see his hair is wet from sweating.

Of course, says Jackson's mom, upstairs to the right.

Dad nods and sort of bows at the same time. Excuse me, he says.

Mom, Jackson says, Sebby wants to spend the night.

His mom looks at both of us.

We'll see, she says. Baby Chester pushes down off her lap then and she lets him go. He starts walking in circles around the coffee table, knocking on it.

Knock-knock, he says. He keeps saying, Knock-knock. Jackson laughs at him and then Baby Chester laughs, too. He goes faster and faster around the table.

Shelly gets up and follows Baby Chester. She's laughing and copying everything he does.

Jackson's mom looks at me. She shakes her head. What am I going to do with them? she whispers.

How old are you? I ask her.

Where did that come from? she asks.

I don't say anything.

I'm thirty-nine, she says. What do you think about that?

That's good, I say, Mother died when she was forty-one years old.

Oh, she says and then looks down at her lap. You must miss her a lot, she tells me.

I lost her picture, I say.

She nods. When Baby Chester runs by her this time, she grabs him and pulls him back up onto her lap. Shelly runs over and climbs on her mom's lap, too.

Jessica Rabbit is hot, Jackson whispers to me. Don't you think so?

I look at the empty plastic mask of Jessica Rabbit's face that's lying on the floor.

Well, I say, she's a cartoon and I don't really like cartoons.

She's hot, says Jackson. He tips back his head and looks at the ceiling.

I'm going to go check on the food, their mom says.

We're eating a turkey for dinner, Shelly tells me. Then she turns around and follows their mom and Baby Chester into the kitchen.

Mom is making another Thanksgiving, since you missed it, says Jackson. He rolls up one of his pant legs. Above his knee, he shows me a very flat, brownish scab. It's an eraser burn, he says.

I reach over and touch his scab with my finger. It's not the kind of scab you can pick.

You erase your skin off until it bleeds, Jackson says. There's a boy who made one three inches long on his arm. We measured it with a ruler.

Jackson pushes his pant leg back down.

It hurts? I ask him.

Sort of, he says.

How come you didn't bring your camera? Jackson asks.

I shrug.

I wanted you to take a picture of me jumping, he says and wipes his nose on his hand. I want it so in the picture you can just see me in the air and it could look like I'm jumping off something really high.

Jackson's mom comes out of the kitchen then.

I think we're just about ready, she says. She looks up the stairs where Dad went. Do you want to go see about your dad? she asks.

I can feel something drop inside of me. My arms and legs and my whole body are heavy and I don't want to move.

Jackson gets up with me and we walk over to the stairs.

Hey, Jackson, his mom says, let Sebby go.

But he keeps walking with me. I look down at his mom. She puts her hands in her pockets and smiles a small, flat smile with her lips pressed together.

The bathroom door is closed.

Dad, I say to the door.

There's no answer.

Dad, I say and I knock. I try to turn the handle and the door opens.

Dad's not inside.

Dad, I say again to nobody. I look behind the shower curtain.

Where is he? Jackson asks.

I don't say anything.

He disappeared? asks Jackson.

I shake my head.

Jackson goes running downstairs.

He disappeared, Jackson's yelling, Sebby's dad disappeared!

I walk down the hallway.

Dad, I say. My voice has gone quiet. I step into the playroom, but I don't see him anywhere.

I go into Jackson's room and open the closet to look inside.

Then I walk into the blue room where Jackson's mom sleeps. I can hear Dad talking. He's talking the words to the song that Van Morrison sings, about girls walking home from school.

Dad, I say. My voice is still quiet.

He doesn't answer me.

I get down on the floor and Dad is under the bed. He looks at me but keeps talking the words to the song.

Dad says the words about leaves falling and falling.

Dad, I say. It's hard to talk. My eyes are burning. Tears are running hot down my cheeks.

Dad, please, I say.

Jackson's mom finds us. She lies down next to me and sees Dad. He's talking the words to the song and not looking at us.

It'll be okay, Jackson's mom says. Then she gets up. Come, she says and reaches her hands down to me.

I let her pull me up and we walk downstairs to the couch. Jackson and Shelly and Baby Chester are sitting, watching TV.

Where is he? asks Jackson.

Their mom doesn't answer.

She says, I want you all to stay right here. Then she goes.

Where is he? Jackson asks me.

Upstairs, I say, and bite the inside of my cheek.

We watch the Nickelodeon show—the one where they dump green slime on people's heads.

Cass is going to meet us at the hospital.

We're in the waiting room. There are rows of chairs and, hanging on the wall, a TV with no sound. I'm holding a bottle of Coke. Jackson's mom gave me a dollar to put in the soda machine. Now the bottle is making my hands cold and I want to throw it away.

I'm watching the door. I see Cass right when she walks in. Her eyes are looking everywhere. When she sees us, she puts up her hand to wave.

I'm Cass, my sister says.

Alison, says Jackson's mom.

Then they hug each other.

His hand is badly bruised, so they've bandaged it and given him pain medication, says Jackson's mom. She looks down at me and then back at Cass. Your father doesn't want to see anyone right now, she says.

Cass bends down to me.

Are you okay? she asks.

I nod yes. It's hard to talk. Cass keeps looking at my eyes. I look away.

Then Cass stands back up and says, You should go. We'll be fine.

All right, says Jackson's mom, call me.

I will, Cass says.

They hug each other again.

Sebastian, says Jackson's mom. Then she doesn't say anything else. She bends down and kisses my forehead before she goes.

Cass sits next to me. Do you want to take your coat off? she asks.

No, I tell her.

I walk over to the garbage can and throw away my bottle of Coke.

In the car I ask Cass, Where are we going?

Home, she says.

But we have to get Cham, I tell her.

Shit, she says, I forgot about the cat.

Cass pulls the car over to the side of the road. She reaches into the backseat for her bag.

I'm sorry, Cass says and pulls out her pack of cigarettes. I watch her light one. She takes it out of her mouth then and looks at it. With her other hand, she rolls down the window a little bit.

I thought he'd be fine at dinner, she says, he seemed better. She holds the tip of her cigarette out the window.

We sit there and Cass smokes her cigarette down until it's small.

Who named the cat, anyway? asks Cass.

I put my hand on the cold window. It leaves a wet handprint.

Dad did, I tell her. Cham is short for champagne, because of the color of his fur.

Oh, she says and flicks her cigarette out the window. Cass pulls the car onto the road again. At the stoplight, she turns around and we drive the other way to go to the white house.

You know, says Cass, Dad has to stay in the hospital for a while. Things are all mixed up in his head and he needs to rest, she says.

I keep looking forward at the long, black road.

When can he get out? I ask her.

I'm not sure, says Cass.

I look out the side window at the tall trees. They're gray and quiet in the dark.

I know where to find the cat. Cass follows me upstairs to the room where Dad sleeps. I turn on the light and see Dad's bed with the covers all messed up. It looks like he's still here. I don't want to touch anything.

Cham, I say to the cat, it's me. I get down on the floor and look under the bed. The cat is sleeping with his head tucked under his tail. I say his name again, but he doesn't wake up, so I crawl underneath and pull him out.

Here, I say and hand him to Cass.

I'll put him in the car, she says, you get your clothes and whatever else you want.

In my room, I pack lots of clothes and also the paper bag from under the bed into my green and blue duffel bag.

The old man holding a dead bird in his hand knows that I'm leaving. In my head, I'm telling him good-bye.

I turn off the light and run downstairs. The front door is open and Cass is standing outside, smoking another cigarette.

I'm going to run up and make sure we're not leaving anything important, Cass says.

Okay, I tell her.

She drops her cigarette on the ground and steps on it.

I stand in the driveway, waiting. Everywhere is dark except for the red tip of Cass's cigarette still glowing. I step on it to squish it all the way out.

Ready? asks Cass. She's running down the front steps.

Yes, I say.

In the car, the cat's meowing and walking back and forth across the backseat.

He never meowed this much before, I say. Dad thought maybe he couldn't.

Well, lucky for us, says Cass, I guess he can. She backs out of the driveway and turns up the radio loud. The cat meows louder.

Fuck it, Cass says and shuts off the radio.

The cat's meows are long and sad. If you really listen, then the sound sort of goes away. I close my eyes and try to sleep.

I was walking in circles around the white house. I could see Mother walking in front of me. She was a girl in a shiny blue nightgown.

I'm tired, I told her.

She kept walking.

Mother, I said, stop.

She turned around the corner and I went to the shed to sleep. I needed to sleep, just for a little bit.

Dear Ms. Lambert,

The song that got stuck in Dad's head is called "Cypress Avenue." Van Morrison says the same words over and over again when he sings and he wears black sunglasses. I asked Mother once if he was blind like Stevie Wonder. She laughed and said no.

We left Dad at the hospital and he has to stay.

I am back home now. I am here with Cass and Leo and the cat, Cham. Please don't tell Katya.

I woke up in the night. I was trying very hard to think about Mother. I wanted to see her in my head, but I was only seeing myself. I saw myself jumping in the water and walking in circles around the white house. Then I stopped looking in my head and I saw my hands petting the cat on my lap. I was there on the floor in my room and now I am here at the kitchen table writing a letter. Mother is farther and farther away from me. I miss her.

Bye, Sebby

PICTURES

Cass is folding laundry on the couch—three piles, one for each of us. On TV, soldiers are riding trucks in Somalia. Cass has been watching all day.

Three hundred thousand people died there in the last year, she tells me again. They're starving. Do you know how many people that is?

I don't answer.

We forgot to bring the yellow bike, I tell her.

She folds a white T-shirt on her lap and then puts it in Leo's pile.

Can I turn it off now? I ask. I don't want to watch the soldiers anymore.

Fine, says Cass. She's quiet and I don't know if she's mad or not. You want a bike? she asks.

I nod.

How about I buy you a new bike if you go back to school? she says.

I think about Ms. Lambert sitting on her desk in the front of the classroom. I think about what's inside my desk: the two sharpened pencils and the purple pencil sharpener and the pack of skinny markers. I think about Katya. Her desk is in the third row and my desk is in the fourth row. I think about all the rows of desks and who sits at them.

Okay, I say to Cass.

Good, she says, it's a deal.

I follow her to the kitchen. She opens the dishwasher and I watch how hot steam comes out.

Then I sit at the table and look at a book that Leo checked out of the library for me. It teaches you how to draw things by mixing easy shapes together. I open the book to a page with a race car track. The race car driver is made out of circles and rectangles.

Hey, says Cass. She puts her hand on my back.

Do you want to go visit Dad on Sunday? she asks.

Yes, I tell her. In my head I count forward to Sunday. Sunday is in four days. We've been home now for almost a whole week.

I was thinking, Cass says, we could make him some cookies. She sits down next to me at the table.

He likes the peanut butter kind, I tell her.

Right, Cass says. She looks at the picture in my book of the race car track. We could make a practice batch today, she says, for Mrs. Alden.

Mrs. Alden is the social worker. She's coming to look at our house and see how we live.

The twelve o'clock news is coming on, says Cass. I want to watch. You stay here and draw, she tells me.

Then we'll make cookies? I ask.

Okay, she says.

Leo drops his heavy red backpack in the hallway and runs to the bathroom. I stand outside the door and listen to him pee and then flush. He doesn't turn on the sink to wash his hands.

Jesus, Leo says when he bumps into me on the way out. What is it? he asks me.

I hand him the peanut butter cookie that I'm holding.

Eat it, I tell him.

Okay, Leo says. He takes a bite.

We walk to the kitchen together and I watch him chew. Cass is sitting at the table, reading her book about where to go to college. She looks up at Leo.

Hey, she says to him, you heard, the troops had no problems so far.

Yeah, says Leo.

Does it taste very good? I ask him. We made them for Dad, I say.

Leo takes one of the tall glasses out of the cabinet and then opens the refrigerator. He holds the cookie in his mouth and pours his glass full of milk.

It's good, Leo says. I like them a little saltier, though. He puts the milk back in the refrigerator and takes out his jar of pickles.

He likes them saltier, I tell Cass.

I heard, she says. She keeps reading her book.

I sit down with Leo.

The cookie's good, he says. Will you stop staring at me now?

Okay, I say. I look at my hands on the table and fold them together like how you pray.

Can you take him to the library with you? Cass asks Leo. I think he needs to get out of the house for a while, she says.

Sure, says Leo. He starts eating his pickles now.

I look at him and then remember not to.

Maybe I'll go to Reed College, Cass says.

Where's that? Leo asks.

Oregon, says Cass.

Shit, Leo says, you're going to go all the way to Oregon?

Cass shrugs and looks back at her book.

Maybe I'll go to Vassar, she says.

Leo doesn't say anything. He closes his jar of pickles and stands up.

Ready to go? he asks me.

I follow him out to the hallway. Leo helps me put on my green coat and he zippers it up, but not all the way to my chin.

See ya, Leo says to Cass.

Bye, she says. I have to go grocery shopping and then I'll come pick you guys up around six.

Outside, our tree in the front yard looks skinny and cold. We walk fast. Leo's wearing a dark blue sweater and no jacket. He walks in front of me with his hands in his pockets. I can see my breath. It's like a tiny cloud in the air and then it disappears. When I breathe out all the hot air from inside of me then I make a bigger cloud that lasts longer.

Are you going to go to college like Cass? I ask Leo.

Yeah, he says.

When are you going to go? I ask.

Leo turns around and looks at me and then faces forward again.

A year and a half, he says, when I finish high school.

Oh, I say. I think about Cass gone and Leo gone, too.

Are you going to go to the same college as Cass? I ask.

No, he says. He starts walking faster now.

I let him get way ahead of me so I have to run to catch up. I keep letting him get ahead and then I run to where he is. Leo turns around.

What're you doing? he asks.

I don't say anything. This time when I catch up, I hold on to the back of his sweater. He lets me hold on the rest of the way to the library.

Inside is really warm. Leo takes off his sweater and then unzips my jacket for me. I follow him to the long table by the window. Leo sits down with his backpack on his lap and after he takes everything out, he reaches up tall and stretches.

I'm going to the kids' room, I tell him.

I find the book that Leo picked for me last time we came. The library has too many books to choose from, so Leo had to pick for me. It's a book called *Mr. Bones,* about a skeleton who's like a normal real person. He walks around his regular house and you can see how all his bones move and work.

I look at Mr. Bones's face and remember how I used to sit in the dark with Mother when her head was hurting. We sat on my bed with the lights off and the shades pulled down.

If I looked at her face for a long time, I could see her bones underneath.

At the end of the book, there's a picture of Mr. Bones standing up tall with his arms hanging down at his sides. His hands are turned out so his palms face forward. All of Mr. Bones's bones are labeled.

On the phone, Ms. Lambert says, Sebby, I would really like it if you came back to school.

I don't know what to say. I look at Cass and hold out the phone for her to take.

You talk, I tell her.

Cass shakes her head no. You, she says.

I put the phone back up to my ear. I can hear Ms. Lambert humming. Her voice sounds pretty.

Talk, Cass tells me.

Ms. Lambert, I say into the phone.

Yes, she says.

What day should I come back? I ask.

Well, says Ms. Lambert, how about if you come next Wednesday? That will give you some time to get ready, she says, and we'll see how the day goes.

Four days, I say.

Right, Ms. Lambert says, Wednesday's in four days.

Where are you? I ask her.

She laughs.

I'm at home, she says.

I don't know where Ms. Lambert's home is or what it looks like.

I'll see you on Wednesday, Ms. Lambert says.

Yes, I tell her.

Good-bye, she says.

Good-bye, I say. I wait for the sound of her hanging up and then I hold out the phone for Cass to take.

The social worker, Mrs. Alden, shakes our hands. Cass's first, then Leo's, then mine. She holds my hand the longest. Mrs. Alden has small, close-together gray eyes and a big, round circle face. I smile at her. Cass told me to keep smiling.

We take her into the family room to sit on the couch. Cass pulls me next to her and Mrs. Alden sits on the other side of me. She smells spicy like gingerbread. Leo's standing up with his hands in his pockets.

Can I get you something to drink, he asks, tea or coffee?

Mrs. Alden says, A glass of water, please.

Cass tells Mrs. Alden that Dad's doing well in the hospital. We're going to see him tomorrow, she says, and Sebby's going back to school on Wednesday. I can give you the school's number, says Cass, if you want to call his teacher—her name is Ms. Lambert.

Leo comes back then with a glass of water and the plateful of peanut butter cookies. He sets them down on the table in front of Mrs. Alden.

Thank you, she says to Leo. I understand you're doing very well in school.

Yes, he says.

And you have some good friends there, I hope? Mrs. Alden asks him.

Leo nods. Some, he says.

Do your friends come over often? she asks.

Not really, says Leo, I get busy with work, you know, lots of homework.

Mrs. Alden take a sip of water. Her lipstick sticks to the glass and makes a pink smile. She turns to me.

Do you want to go back to school, Sebastian? she asks.

I know what to say. Yes, I tell her, I like my teacher.

I watch how Mrs. Alden's hand reaches forward and breaks off a piece of peanut butter cookie. She has small, pink hands with clean fingernails. I like how her hands look.

Cass pats my back two times.

Do you want to see my room? I ask Mrs. Alden.

Sure, she says and smiles at me without showing her teeth.

Mrs. Alden holds on to the railing and goes slow up the stairs. I wait for her at the top. In my room, I show her my toys. The wooden cars and the wooden blocks for building things and my card games.

Mrs. Alden asks me if I like to read books.

I show her the book *What Do People Do All Day?* She sits down with me on the bed and I turn the pages so she can see the pictures.

Do you have a favorite page? she asks.

I shake my head, no.

I used to look at all the pictures every night before I went to bed, I tell her.

Mrs. Alden nods. I like to read at night, too, she says, it helps me sleep.

Her spicy gingerbread smell is getting all over my room, but that's okay. It's a good smell. I look at the loose skin under her chin and I think it would feel soft and nice to touch.

At the library, I read the Mr. Bones book, I say.

Oh, says Mrs. Alden, I don't know that one—is it good?

Yes, I tell her, Mr. Bones stands like this.

I get up to show her how Mr. Bones stands with his arms by his sides and his palms facing out.

He has lines pointing all over him that say the names of his bones, I tell her. I look at my watch. It says 2:46 PM.

I tell Mrs. Alden, it's two-forty-six.

Do you want to go back downstairs? she asks.

Yes, I say. I follow her out of my room and walk behind her down the steps. We go really slowly.

Cass and Leo are waiting for me there at the bottom.

I want to take the cat with us to visit Dad, but Cass says no. She says the hospital won't let us.

Besides that, she says, Cham hates the car.

I sit in the middle of the backseat. I'm holding the plate of cookies wrapped in tinfoil on my lap. I put my hand on the warm tinfoil.

In the car, we don't talk very much.

Well, Cass says and then she doesn't say anything else. She puts on the news radio and turns down the volume so you can't really hear the voices talking.

I bet we could've brought the cat in a bag and snuck him in, says Leo.

Yes, I say.

Shit, Cass says to Leo, you don't know how loud that cat can be.

At the hospital, Cass drives around the parking lot twice and then parks in the last row, away from all the other cars. We just sit for a minute. Leo gets out first and then I get out. I'm holding the plate of cookies. The tinfoil is shining bright in my eyes.

Cass walks close to me with her hand on my back, and inside, she pushes me with her to a high desk where there's a woman wearing light blue hospital clothes. I look back at Leo. He's staring down at his feet.

Stephen Lane, says Cass.

Yes, says the woman and she takes us to a blue room.

Dad's sitting on a soft, blue chair. His bad hand is wrapped in a bandage and his beard is shaved off. His face looks soft and new like a baby face.

Cass pulls me over to the blue couch with her. I hold the plate of cookies on my lap. We look at Leo standing by the door, biting his lip. He comes and sits down next to me.

It's good to see you guys, Dad says.

Yeah, says Leo. He leans forward and grabs a very green plastic plant off the table in front of us. He shakes it and then laughs at it.

We miss you, Cass tells Dad.

Leo's holding the plastic plant on his lap, pinching and poking at its leaves. What's the point of these things? he asks. I mean, everyone knows they're fake, he says.

Dad leans back in his blue chair and puts his feet up on the table. He's not wearing any shoes, but he has on clean white socks.

I've gained seven pounds, Dad says, and I'm feeling better.

That's great, says Cass. She lets go of my hand.

I'm staring at Dad's feet. I want to touch his new socks. I want to sit with Dad in his soft blue chair. I want to touch his new face.

Sebby's going back to school, says Cass. She looks up at the ceiling. This lighting is terrible, she says.

Dad looks up at the ceiling, too. He shrugs, then looks at me.

Good for you, he says, I'm proud of you.

I bring him the plate of cookies and he peels back the tinfoil.

Wow, he says.

This lighting makes skin greenish, Cass says. She's holding out her arm, looking at her skin.

We're in a goddamn hospital, says Leo, what do you expect?

Cass turns to him and rolls her eyes. He's still holding the plastic plant on his lap.

Then I jump on Dad. A big puff of air and a low noise comes out of him.

Sebby! Cass yells at me. She stands up. What are you doing? she says. You have to be careful.

I'm okay, Dad says. He holds up his bad hand and puts his elbow down on the big arm of the chair. Dad's breath smells like toothpaste.

I scoot back into his lap and that makes the plate of cookies fall.

Shit, Cass says. Sebby, for Christ's sake.

Cass gets down on the floor to clean up. She sets the plate on the table and starts picking up pieces of cookie, putting them back on the plate. Dad tries to lean forward to help her, but he can't really, because I'm on his lap.

Cass says, I got it, Dad.

I put my hand on Dad's cheek. It feels soft and cool.

Dad, I say, do you want to come home with us now? The cat is at home, I tell him.

He can't, says Leo. He puts the plant back on the table and moves it so it's in the right place.

How's the cat? Dad asks me.

Good, I say.

Dad's watching Leo.

How you doing? Dad asks him.

Fine, Leo says, school's fine, everything's fine.

There's a knock on the door and then it opens. The woman in blue hospital clothes smiles and tells us the visit is half over. She closes the door again and leaves us alone.

You know about Somalia? Cass asks.

Yes, says Dad, Operation Restore Hope.

At the bike store, I pick out a green ten-speed. The green paint sparkles like the kind of sidewalk that has pieces of glass mixed in.

Good choice, says Leo.

The bike store man takes it off the rack for me. He says, Do you want to try it in the parking lot?

I tell him no.

Are you sure? he asks.

I nod at him. He's wearing the tight kind of clothes for riding bikes, so I can see how big his muscles are.

Leo finds a green and brown camouflage helmet. He puts it on me and tightens the straps. Then he knocks on my head three times. Knock, knock, knock. I can't feel anything.

I'm putting all my pictures in a red photo album. This was Ms. Lambert's idea. She said that if I wanted to, I could make an album and then bring in my pictures to show her. She called this morning to make sure I'm going back to school tomorrow, because tomorrow is Wednesday. It has been four days.

All of my pictures only fill up seven pages, I tell Cass. I counted and the album has fifty pages.

You can take more, Cass says.

I walk around the house to see if I want to take more pictures or not. I try to look for bright spots where Mother touched that haven't been touched by anyone else yet. If I can find a bright spot, then I will take more pictures.

I'm looking all over. They're hard to find. I look in Mother's room and inside her closet. I look in Mother's bathroom and then I find one on the tile wall above the bathtub. It's big, the size of a whole handprint.

I get my camera and take a picture of the bright spot. I write the time, 3:14 PM, and the date, December 12.

Cass! I yell.

In here, she says. She's sitting at the kitchen table reading her college book.

Now I have to take a picture of your face, I tell her.

She puts her book down on her lap.

Okay, she says. Smiling or not?

Just regular, I tell her.

The square photo comes out of the camera and I shake it dry. I write, Cass, 3:22 PM, December 12.

I know it's almost time for Leo to be home. I stand by the door with my camera, ready to take a picture of his face. I have to wait and wait, so in my head I think of more pictures to take: Mother's shoes in her closet, Leo's messy bed, the place in the backyard where I buried the piece of Styrofoam.

Then I hear Leo coming. He opens the door and I take a picture.

Hey, he says, what's going on?

In the picture, Leo's looking up at the ceiling. His face is red from the cold outside.

The classroom is decorated for winter with blue and white paper snowflakes hanging from the ceiling. When I left, it was still decorated for fall.

There's a card for me in my desk. The card has flowers and a tree on it—the kind that Mica draws. She's the best artist, so the drawing is very good and all the coloring-in is neat. In blue letters, the card says, Welcome Back, and inside it says, We Missed YOU! Everyone in class had to write their name. Katya wrote her name like a rainbow with every letter a different color. Ms. Lambert wrote in black pen and drew a little cat face.

The card makes me feel bad. I want to rip up Mica's flowers and her tree, too. I want to rip up all the names of everyone in class. I hide the card at the bottom of my desk.

Come on, Katya says. She's waiting for me by the door.

We walk to the cafeteria for lunch and sit together at one of the long tables.

Are you okay? she asks me. She brushes down the back of my hair with her hand.

I don't answer.

Since we can't play outside in the snow, half of the cafeteria is for eating and board games and the other half is for running and playing with balls. The room is too loud and the lights shining down make the floor very bright. I want to cover my ears and duck under the table to hide from all the balls flying around.

The girl named Jessica comes and stands in front of me.

Why were you gone? she asks. She has a purple fruit roll-up wrapped around one of her fingers.

Leave him alone, says Katya.

Jessica puts her fruit roll-up finger in her mouth and stares at us.

Go away, Katya tells her.

What, is he your baby? asks Jessica. When he cries do you hug him and kiss him and hold him like a baby? She turns around then and goes away. Her long blond hair hangs all the way down her back.

Katya's eating pieces of apple. She eats all the white part off and then puts the green skins back in her plastic Baggie. I look in my lunch and take out my turkey sandwich. The mayonnaise made the bread get mushy, so I carry it over to the brown trash can and drop it in.

Hello, says the lunch-duty lady who watches everyone eat.

Hi, I say. I don't look up at her. I know what she looks like. She has gray hair that sticks out in two sharp pigtails.

I'm glad you came back, she tells me.

I nod at her legs. She's wearing big pants that have red flowers all over them.

I go sit down next to Katya and open my bag of chips.

Can I have one? she asks me.

I hold out the bag to her and she takes more than one. I think about the card hiding in the bottom of my desk. I know it's there. I want to rip up Katya's rainbow name.

You're okay? asks Katya.

Leave me alone, I say and I walk away. I walk out of the cafeteria and back to Ms. Lambert's room. The door is open, so I go in. Ms. Lambert's not there. Nobody's there.

I take the card out of my desk and put it in the trash can at the front of the room. I look at the card in the trash and then I take it out. I rip it up into pieces. More and more pieces. I keep ripping it up.

Cass is waiting for me on the front steps.

How was school? she asks.

I lean my bike against the house.

I'm tired, I say. I want to be by myself in my room.

Are you hungry? asks Cass.

I do feel hungry, but I want to be by myself. Not now, I tell her.

I go upstairs to my room and close the door. Then I sit down on the floor. I take my photo album out of my backpack and look at all the pictures.

When I close my eyes and lie down, I can see all the pictures in my head, and even though I lost it, I can see the picture of Mother's face laughing. I can see her for as long as I want.

Sebby, says Cass's voice.

I don't say anything. I open my eyes and watch the door open.

Here, Cass says. She puts the cat down on the floor and then leaves. The cat's looking at me.

I pat my chest twice to tell him to come. He steps up onto my chest and pushes his face into my chin. I close my eyes and I can see Mother. Her face is happy.

The cat lets me pick him up. I carry him over to my bed and he sits next to me with his head resting on my leg. I read *The Guinness Book of World Records.* I'm on page 22, the part about Largest Bones.

At school, I have to take a break. I go to the girls' bathroom because the boys don't flush, so their bathroom smells bad. If you don't hold your breath in there then the smell gets stuck in the back of your throat.

I look around to make sure nobody's watching. Then I listen and I don't hear any sounds inside so I pull open the door and I can see the bathroom's empty. I run to the stall all the way at the back and lock myself in. It's echoey quiet. What I do is stand up on the toilet so my feet don't show, take off my glasses, and push my forehead against the cold tile wall. In the girls' bathroom, the tiles are pink and yellow. My eyes are closed so I can't see the pink and yellow, but I know the colors are there.

I think of a song. I think of the song "Crimson and Clover" and I make the words come into my head so I can hear them. Then I stop pushing my forehead against the tile and I feel light inside, like I am the song. I am just the song.

I have my pencil in my hand. I take a folded-up piece of paper out of my pocket and hold it against the wall. I write, My head is a camera.

Dear Ms. Lambert,

If I make my head like a camera, then I can see Mother. I see the picture of her that I lost. I know time is going, but in my head, I can make time stop still.

Mother felt time going away from her. I know how Mother walked in circles around the white house. She walked forward for two hours and then backward for two hours. Then forward again and then backward. The backward circles were to erase the forward circles. She wanted to start over.

I feel time like it's growing and growing bigger, like there is so much time and the time keeps pulling me farther away from Mother. But, if my head is a camera, I can make Mother stay. I can make her hold still. And then it is okay for me to be here with Dad and Cass and Leo. I can be here in all of this time.

Bye, Sebby

I don't want to go outside for morning recess.

Katya says, Are you coming?

No, I tell her, you go.

I sit at my desk and eat my Cheerios. Ms. Lambert's at the front of the room, looking at the chalkboard. She erases the part of the morning schedule that we've already done. Then she comes over. She stands in front of me and puts her hands on my desk. I look at her hands. Her fingernails are a little bit long and not painted any color.

She asks, Did you remember to bring your camera?

I take it out of my backpack and show it to her.

Great, says Ms. Lambert.

I ask her can I take a picture of her face.

Sure, she says. She stands there in front of me with her hands on my desk and smiles a nice, small smile for the picture.

Ms. Lambert says, I think you will be okay here, Sebby. Do you think so?

I think so, I tell her.

I feel very lucky that you've told me so many things in your letters, she says and brushes back my hair with her fingers.

I look at her gold necklace that has a tiny horseshoe on it.

I have something to tell everyone, she says, but I wanted to tell you first.

What is it? I ask.

I'm pregnant, says Ms. Lambert, I'm going to have a baby in the spring. She takes her black and white Chap Stick out of her pocket and puts it on her lips.

I look at her stomach. I can't see it, I tell her.

She laughs. No, she says, not yet, but look. She walks over to her desk and brings back a shadowy black-and-white picture.

That's the baby, she says and points.

It looks like a strawberry, I tell her.

She smiles and nods.

Then Katya comes in early from recess. She says, I'm very boring.

You mean you're very bored? Ms. Lambert asks.

Katya nods and comes over to my desk.

That's your camera? she asks.

Yes, I say.

I let her pick it up and look at it.

Do you want a picture of me now? she asks.

Okay, I say, but I don't like you to act like I'm your baby.

I'm sorry, Katya tells me.

This time the lady wearing hospital clothes takes us to a yellow room. She holds the door open for us to go in. Cass goes first and then Leo and I.

Dad's sitting in a rocking chair next to a yellow couch. He puts his hand up to wave.

I'm coming home, Dad says, on the twenty-second. He's rocking slow in his chair.

Oh my God, says Cass and she runs over to hug him.

I count the days in my head.

Five days, I say.

I guess so, he says, and nods. Five days.

Dad, Cass says, this is great. Her voice is happy and loud.

I'm sure Christmas will be awesome, says Leo. He doesn't look at Dad or anyone.

Don't be an asshole, Cass tells him.

Dad puts up his hands. He doesn't have the bandage on anymore.

It's okay, Dad says.

Cass goes and sits on the couch. I sit next to her, but Leo keeps standing by the door.

I'm sorry, Dad says, about all of this.

Dad, says Cass, but then her voice stops and it's quiet.

Do you still smell good? I ask Dad.

Cass and Dad both laugh.

They keep me very clean here, he says.

I get up and go to him. I sit on his lap and put my head on his shoulder. I can smell the clean smell on his neck.

Why do you have this on? Dad asks and pulls on my backpack.

He won't take it off, Cass says. He sleeps with it.

My album's inside, I tell him, all my pictures.

Oh, Dad says. His breath smells minty.

But he won't show anybody, Cass tells him.

Hmmm, Dad says and that makes warm air come out of his nose.

I touch the skin there above his lip. My finger fits between the bumps of skin that go down from his nose to his mouth. Dad pulls my finger away from his face. Then he holds my hand and squeezes it tight.

On the phone, Jackson says he's coming to visit for Christmas. His Mom and Shelly and Baby Chester are coming, too. I listen and when Jackson stops talking, I hand the phone back to Cass for her to hang up.

Now what are we going to do for dinner? Cass asks me. She goes over and opens the refrigerator. It hums and breathes out cold air. Cass makes a clicking sound with her tongue while she looks.

Did the doctor take a picture of the baby inside Mother's stomach? I ask.

What? says Cass. She looks at me and pushes the refrigerator closed with her foot.

I want to see the picture of Sara Rose and put it in my album, I tell her.

Sebby, Cass says, why? Why would you want that? She was never born, Cass says in an angry voice. We never even knew her.

I want to know her picture, I say.

She walks over to me. I don't understand, she says. Her voice is quiet now.

I want to see the picture, I tell her again.

Stop, Cass says. She steps closer. Her face is too close to my face. I look down, away from her eyes.

Look at me, Cass says. Her voice is loud again and she shakes my shoulders. I can't move. I can't make my eyes look at her.

What's wrong with you? she asks. Why don't you think about other people?

Cass lets go of me and I step backward. She sits down and looks out the window.

You don't think, Cass says to the window. The window is dark, dark blue because it's almost night.

I don't understand, says Cass. She talks to the window like I'm not here anymore.

Our tree in the front yard is white now and thicker with snow. I sit down on the big rock in the dead garden that used to be Mother's and I wait. I'm waiting for a cab to bring Dad home.

Cass opens the front door and says, Sebby? She sees me sitting on the big rock. It's too cold to sit outside, she says and then she comes out and stands next to me.

Leo's not waiting for Dad to come home. He's upstairs in his room reading a book called *The Origin of Species* by Charles Darwin. Leo told me this book is about how we evolved from a tiny speck of life.

I asked him, What's a tiny speck of life?

Like an amoeba, a one-celled organism, he said. Life started in the water and then slowly, slowly made its way onto land. He showed me a picture of a turtle crawling out of the ocean and onto a beach. Leo said, Dad is the turtle. I keep thinking about Dad being a turtle.

Cass blows a bubble with the piece of pink gum she's chewing. Her bubble gets almost as big as her whole face.

How'd you do that? I ask her. She pops the bubble and pushes the gum back into her mouth.

Four pieces of gum at once, Cass says. She puts her hand on my head. I quit smoking, she tells me.

Why? I ask.

She lifts up her foot so she's balancing on the other one. Her hand's still on my head and feels heavier now.

Because, Cass says, Dad didn't like it and it was harder to breathe. She puts her foot back down and lifts up the other one. Her hand feels lighter and then heavier again.

I think there's something wrong with my lungs, says Cass, Maybe they're too small or something. You know, she says, like how some people have a small bladder?

I don't say anything. Cass stomps her feet on the ground.

My legs are going numb, she says.

I'm not cold, I tell her.

Cass starts humming. I don't know what song her voice is making.

I tell her, Shhhhhh, listen. I can hear a car sound coming. We're quiet and the sound gets louder and then I can see the black-and-white Checker cab. It turns into our driveway and I run over to where it stops. Dad gets out of the backseat and hands the driver some money. Then Dad picks me up. I wrap my legs around him tight and hold on. Cass comes over now, too. She gives Dad a hug and I am there in the middle. It's nice and warm.

The driver gets a blue duffel bag out of the trunk.

I got it, says Cass and she takes the bag from him.

We walk to the house. I'm holding on tight to Dad so he won't put me down. Over his shoulder, I watch the black-and-white cab go backward down our driveway and out onto the street. I watch it drive away.

Cass holds the door open and then locks the latch behind us. She sets Dad's blue duffel bag on the couch.

Dad's home! she yells up the stairs to Leo.

Dad walks with me into the kitchen and back out to the TV room. He looks in the downstairs bathroom and then he looks upstairs. I rest my head on his shoulder and Dad walks around the house, seeing everything again. Then he sits down on the couch and I am there on his lap.

Cass sits down on the couch, too.

Dad says, Albert King died last night.

I smell Dad's minty breath.

The blues guy? asks Cass.

Yeah, says Dad, I heard it on the radio in the cab.

Leo comes in with his fat book under his arm.

How'd he die? Leo asks. He sits down on the floor and puts his elbows up on the coffee table.

I think they said heart failure, says Dad.

Leo nods.

Your mother saw Albert King once at the Blues Festival in Newport, Dad says. I wish I'd been there with her.

Where were you? I ask him.

I wasn't there, he says, I don't know where I was.

I look at the soft spot of skin under Dad's chin. I reach up and touch it with my finger.

Stop, that tickles, he says and grabs my hand away. He wipes his face with his sleeve. Then he looks up at the ceiling and yawns. Albert King is dead, Dad whispers.

I wake up in the night and walk to the room that's just Dad's room now. Dad is sleeping on his side of the bed with the covers all kicked off and the cat curled up by his feet. He's wearing new white socks from the hospital. They're bright in the dark.

I lie down next to him and put my hand on his chest. I close my eyes. It's okay to close my eyes because I can feel Dad next to me. I can feel his chest breathing up and down, up and down. I count in my head until I fall back asleep.

The room is full of light. Dad's not with me anymore and the cat's gone, too. Someone put the covers back on the bed and tucked me in underneath. I can hear the TV on downstairs and Cass's voice talking loud.

You don't know what you're doing! Cass yells. Those are Mom's private things and you can't just give them to him like they're nothing!

I wait for Dad's voice. I wait and then I can hear the sound of Dad's voice, but I can't hear the words he's saying.

I get up and stand in front of the mirror in the bathroom. Today is Saturday. I know that today at two o'clock I'm supposed to ride my bike to the playground at school to meet Katya. Tomorrow, Jackson and Shelly are coming.

I put my face very close to the mirror so I can see better, because I'm not wearing my glasses.

Hello, I say to my face. My breath makes the mirror foggy wet. I wipe it dry with the sleeve of my pajama shirt.

Sebby, says Dad's voice.

I'm in here, I tell him.

Dad comes and stands in the bathroom doorway.

I have something for you, he says. He turns and goes into the bedroom and I follow.

Cass told me, says Dad. I found this for you. He picks up a brown yellow envelope sitting on the dresser. He opens it and shows me.

This one is you, he says.

The picture is black and gray and I know what it is. It's a picture of me inside of Mother's stomach.

This one is your sister, Dad says. He lays the pictures on the bed for me to look at.

I bend over close so I can see more. On the bottom of both is a piece of white-colored tape. The pieces of tape say, Sebastian at two months and Sara Rose at two months.

She looks like me, I tell Dad.

He reaches out his hand and touches the top of my head. Then he puts both of his hands in his pockets and stands like that, looking at me.

The pictures make me think of my photo album.

Where is it?

I have the question in my head, but the words are stuck.

Dad says, What's the matter?

Then I ask him. I say the words, Where is it?

Dad scrunches his face. What? he asks.

I run past him into my room. My backpack is there, a lump under the covers on my bed. I dig it out and my album is still inside. I have to look at all the pages and count the pictures to make sure everything's right. Dad's watching me with his arms crossed in front of his chest. I can see him watching me even though I'm not looking at him.

Then Dad leaves me. I'm alone and I count twenty-six pictures in my album. That's the right number. I feel better. I close my eyes and tell myself I am okay.

I hear three quick knocks on my door.

Sebby? says Dad.

I'm okay, I say.

He comes in and hands me the new pictures.

I want to tell you something, says Dad, it's very important. He stops talking.

What? I ask.

My glasses are on the little table next to my bed. I reach over and put them on.

The baby died before your mother, he says. Three days before. The baby died inside your mother's stomach.

No, I tell Dad, the baby was with her when she ran into the lights.

The lights? Dad asks.

The car, I tell him.

No, Sebby, Dad says, Mother lost the baby three days before the car. We didn't tell you because there was just too much, Dad says, too many things. He stops talking again.

Why did the baby die? I ask.

Something happened, an accident inside your mother's body, says Dad. It's called a miscarriage.

I don't say anything.

Dad sits down next to me on my bed.

Mother was by herself running and then she ran into the car? I ask.

The car hit her, says Dad, I don't know how it happened. The driver said she came out of nowhere.

I sit very still and think about Mother and the baby. Sara

Rose wasn't inside of Mother, watching, when the car came. Mother was alone when she died.

Come on, Dad says.

I close my album, zip up my backpack, and pull it on. Dad stands up and then helps me off my bed. On the way downstairs, he puts his hand on my backpack and I like that.

Cass and Leo are sitting at the table. Leo's working with his different-colored folders everywhere and Cass is reading one of his books about math.

Leo looks at me and nods.

Hey, says Cass, I saved you some French toast if you want it.

I sit down at the table.

I hated calculus, Cass says and pushes Leo's math book over to him. Then she scoots back in her chair and gets up. Milk? she asks me.

Yes, I tell her.

I turn around and look at Dad. He's standing there, very tall behind my chair. I tell him to sit.

Oh, he says and pulls out the chair next to mine.

Hey, Cass, says Dad, where'd I put my coffee?

I don't know, she says. She opens a cabinet and takes out a black coffee cup. It makes a clinking noise when she puts it down on the counter. Here, she says, start a new one.

Dad gets up and I watch him pour the coffee.

Maybe we could go for a drive later today, Dad says. There's that lake where people ice-skate.

Dear Ms. Lambert,

Dad is home. Now everyone is here, but Mother is not.

I have to tell you what happened to Mother, because I know. First, the baby died in Mother's stomach. Then she went running by herself in the night. A car came around the corner with its lights shining. Mother closed her eyes and she ran into the lights.

Dad said, We still have to be a family. He took us to the lake. It was dark when we got there. Leo was sleeping with his head back and his mouth open. Dad woke him up. It was dark outside, but there were tall yellow lights. Cass put on her skates and we watched her. She skated in loops like the number 8. Then Leo went on the ice in his shoes. He doesn't have skates. Dad and I don't either. Leo tried to skate in his shoes. It was funny. Then Dad tried to do it, too. Cass held my hands and pulled me onto the ice.

Mother is not here. She's a picture in my head. She's laughing with her eyes closed.

I fell asleep on the way home. I lay down across the backseat and Leo held my feet on his lap. When we got home, Dad carried me inside. I was awake, because I could hear things, but I didn't open my eyes. The cat was meowing.

Dad said, Will somebody feed the cat?

I got it, Cass said.

Dad carried me upstairs and I could feel my chest getting warmer and warmer and I knew that was all of the life inside of me.

I'm going to live for a very long time.

Dad tucked me into bed and I pretended to be asleep and then I really was asleep.

Now it's Christmas Eve morning. Merry Christmas to you.

Bye, Sebby

Cass brings in a big, white tray with a tinfoil cover.

What is it? I ask her.

I think it's a ham, she says.

Jackson's mom comes in after Cass with another tray.

They're carrying stuff in from the van. Dad's in the kitchen moving everything around to make more room. He brought the toaster and the blender and all the kitchen plants out here and set them on the couch in front of the TV.

Is that everything now? Dad asks Cass.

Almost, she tells him.

Jackson and Shelly are riding their bikes in circles around the driveway. I have to get my bike from behind the house, but I'm looking at the toaster and the blender and all the kitchen plants sitting on the couch. They look funny there, like they want me to turn on the TV so they can watch.

It's okay, Cass says, go get your bike.

Cass gives me a little push on the back and I go to where my bike is behind the house. I put on my helmet and ride to the front. Jackson and Shelly are waiting for me.

Where can we go? asks Jackson.

I start riding to school since I know the way. Jackson and Shelly follow behind me. I pedal fast and do all the turns without slowing down.

At school, we ride in fast circles around the blacktop where there are the basketball hoops and also the tetherball poles. Jackson rides standing up high on his pedals. I don't try to do that. Jackson can also let go of his handlebars. He holds up his arms above his head like a bad guy, and yells, Don't shoot, don't shoot!

Jackson does a sideways skid stop and drops his bike onto the ground.

Show off! Shelly yells at him.

I stop my bike next to Jackson. Shelly keeps riding in circles.

This is your school? asks Jackson.

I nod and get off my bike.

You got a small playground, he says. He runs over to the red-and-white painted merry-go-round. Some of the paint's scraped off so you can see the gray metal underneath. I like to touch the metal with my fingertip and feel how it's cold.

Jackson sits down in the middle of the merry-go-round.

Push me, he says.

I hold on to one of the bars and run around as fast as I can and then let go. Jackson lies down with his arms up and out so he looks like a big spinning letter X.

Shelly comes running over. You're going to get sick! she yells at Jackson.

She grabs on to one of the bars and lets the merry-go-round drag her until it stops. Jackson stands up.

Damn it, he says, you leave me alone.

He barfs every time, Shelly says to me.

Shut up! Jackson screams. He jumps down off the merry-go-round and pushes past us.

I watch him walk over to the rope ladder and climb to the top.

Last time, Shelly says in a low voice, he threw up his whole pack of sour gummy worms.

She's standing close and I can feel her voice coming out on my neck. Her voice feels warm.

Then he started crying, says Shelly, because he said it wasn't fair and he wanted more gummy worms to eat, but Mom said no.

I don't say anything. I'm watching Jackson at the top of the slide. He's standing up there looking around.

I got an idea! Jackson shouts at us. He slides down.

Come on, he says.

I follow him back to the bikes. Jackson gets on and starts riding fast. I look at Shelly. She's still on the playground.

Come on, I tell her, hurry.

We ride across the dead grass field all the way to the brown wooden fence. Behind the fence is an apartment building with rows of balconies that all look the same. I've counted and I know the building has twenty-four balconies.

How do we get over? asks Jackson.

You have to go the other way from outside of school, I tell him.

Let's go, he says.

I ride back over the field and the blacktop, out of school. Jackson and Shelly are behind me.

I stop in front of the driveway where you go into the

building. There's a small parking lot and also a swimming pool with a fence around it. Jackson rides past me to the pool and pushes open the gate.

Look, he says. Jackson goes in with his bike and the gate slams shut behind him. He starts riding around the pool in fast circles. He goes faster and faster.

If you fall in, then you die, says Jackson. Come on.

I walk my bike over to the gate. I try to open it, but the gate's locked now. The handle won't turn.

Jackson skid-stops and opens the gate for me and Shelly. The pool water is low down with a blue cover over it. The cover's not moving and I don't know if the water is ice or not.

I don't want to, says Shelly.

Jackson looks at me.

Why're you wearing your backpack? he asks.

Because it's important, I tell him.

He doesn't say anything.

I get on my bike and ride slow around the pool. Jackson rides fast and when he passes by, his wind pushes me backward hard, but doesn't tip me over.

Stop it, Shelly yells at us, stop! I want to go. Sebby, she yells, please, I want to go now! Sebby! she yells my name again.

I stop my bike next to her and get off. We watch Jackson going fast around the pool.

We're leaving, Shelly yells at him, and you don't know the way back! Let's go, she says to me.

I look at her.

He's just showing off, she says, he'll come.

We walk our bikes out and the gate slams shut. Jackson's not stopping and he's not looking at us. He keeps riding around the pool.

Go, Shelly yells at me, go!

I start riding. When I look back, Shelly's there following, but Jackson's not.

Good, Shelly says, faster.

I keep going and I don't look back anymore. I ride like it's just me riding home by myself. I ride looking up at the skinny, stick trees.

Then I hear Jackson's voice yelling behind me.

Screw you guys! he yells. I could've fallen in and died! What if I died! he yells.

You idiot! Shelly screams at him.

I don't look back.

Dad and Cass and Leo are sitting in the kitchen with Jackson's mom. Baby Chester's sleeping on the floor in his car seat. I watch how Jackson's mom rocks the seat back and forth with her foot. Today she's wearing red socks.

You're home fast, Dad says to us. He's holding a carrot and takes a loud bite.

On the table, there's a big silver platter that has carrots and celery and cauliflower and in the middle is a bowl of white dip.

How was the ride? asks Dad.

I look at Jackson and Shelly standing next to me. Shelly goes over to her mom and hugs her around the neck.

It was fine, Jackson says.

Good, says Dad.

I pull on the collar of my coat to stretch it away from my neck.

You guys can take off your warm stuff and play, Cass says. Why don't you show them your room, Sebby?

I walk out of the kitchen then and unzip my coat. I let it fall down on the floor by the couch. Jackson and Shelly drop their coats next to mine.

We go upstairs and sit on the floor in my room. I dig my hands down into the scratchy brown carpet.

I know a joke, I say.

What is it? asks Jackson. He takes off his green sweater. Underneath he's wearing a blue turtleneck.

Why don't skeletons fight each other? I say.

I don't know, says Shelly.

Because, I say, they don't have any guts.

I get it, Shelly says, I get it! She's smiling.

I've never heard that one before, says Jackson. He smiles a little bit. Do you have toys? he asks.

In the trunk over in the corner I have my wooden toys, not the kind he would like. I don't say anything.

Let's hide, says Shelly.

I nod, yes. I already know where to go.

Where? Jackson asks.

I get my orange flashlight out from under my bed. Jackson and Shelly come with me into Dad's room. I open the closet and feel for the handle of the secret door.

It's called a crawl space, I say.

Mother told me this was the best place to hide in the whole house.

I remember she waited for me to get home from school and she said, Let's disappear. We hid together and she held my hand in the dark. All the noise in her head went away.

We won't come out, she said, until we're sure they miss us.

Mother felt like she was disappearing and I felt like I was growing. She let go of my hand and I was everywhere in the dark.

Woah, Jackson says, cool.

I point my flashlight so we can see.

Shelly pushes Jackson in first and then I go. Shelly comes in last. We sit, not talking. I point my flashlight straight up at the low ceiling and the light shines back down on us.

I listen to Dad's voice talking downstairs. I listen and wait to hear Leo's voice and Cass's voice, too. They're happy, sitting around the table. Dad's face is warm, I know, and his ears are red from laughing. Their voices make me safe.

When Jackson pulls the short door all the way shut, I can't hear the voices talking to each other anymore, but I know they're still there.

Turn the light off, Jackson says.

I turn off my orange flashlight and the dark is so dark I can't see Jackson or Shelly. I can't see my legs or my arms or my hands. Shelly puts her hand on my face. She spreads her fingers out on my cheek and holds her hand like that so she can know I'm still here. I listen to the quiet and I hear Jackson's nose sniffling. The dark is dark like the inside of my head. I can see Jackson like he's a picture. I can see him wiping his nose on the back of his hand, but really, I can't see him at all.

Shelly giggles. I like this, she says.

Shh, Jackson tells her.

I think about how I want to be here, where I am right now.

In the dark my body is growing, filling up space so that I can reach all the way to where Mother is. My chest is big and warm. I can feel time, my whole life stretching out and out.

I know what to do. Tomorrow and the next day and the day after that. I'll take more pictures and my album will fill up.

I promise, Mother, I'll remember everything.

ACKNOWLEDGMENTS

I want to thank my family—especially my parents, Bill and Randi Brinkman, and my grandmother, Arlyne Geschwender—for their constant love and support and for raising me on good music.

Many thanks to my incredibly dedicated editor, Elisabeth Schmitz, and everyone at Grove/Atlantic. I am indebted to my agent, Alice Tasman, who has read this book as many times as I have and whose enthusiasm and encouragement never wane.

I am always grateful for Keith Hedlund, who believed in me from the very beginning.

A warm thank-you to my generous and talented teacher, Maud Casey, for all her thoughtful advice. A big thank-you to Cristina Garcia for her kindness and support. And, my gratitude to Alison Smith for guiding me through numerous revisions.

Thanks to Dave Eggers for taking a new writer seriously and continually finding the time to read my work.

Many thanks to Rebecca Brown, Paul Selig, and my fellow writers and friends at Goddard College, especially Jen Eriksen, Ross Brown, Alexis Smith, Sarah Edrie, Tifa Boss, and Elaine Livingstone.

Thank you to all the children at San Francisco's Up On Top Afterschool Program for surprising and inspiring me every day, especially Drew Connery. And thanks to Drew's wonderful grandmother, Ann Connery.

Also, thank you to Zack Montague for showing me how to experience the world in new ways—and thank you to his parents, Valerie Montague and Steve Kravitz.

Finally, I want to thank my friends, many of whom have read and reread my work: Augusta Meill, Hamish Chandra, Alyson Sena, Liz Anderson, Emily Benz, John Scopelleti, Laura Steuble, Julie Popkin, Susan Campbell, Ruiyan Xu, Aimee Lee, the Hannum family, and the Grasso family.

Up High in the Trees

Kiara Brinkman

ABOUT THIS GUIDE

We hope that these discussion questions
will enhance your reading group's exploration
of Kiara Brinkman's *Up High in the Trees*. They are
meant to stimulate discussion, offer new viewpoints,
and enrich your enjoyment of the book.

More reading group guides and additional information,
including summaries, author tours, and author sites for
other fine Grove Press titles, may be found on
our Web site, www.groveatlantic.com.

QUESTIONS FOR DISCUSSION

1. How would you describe the voice of Sebby, the narrator? Does he seem troubled, perhaps as a result of the early loss of his mother, or something else? Does his voice sound erratic and unstable to you, or is he particularly alert and sensitive? As you get to know him, is he so different from other bright, strong-minded, lonely eight-year-olds? Would you agree it is a powerful and always honest voice we hear?

2. When does Sebby take responsibility for others' welfare? Think of his caring for his father's feet, his aiding Shelly, and nurturing the cat. Other times? On the other hand, Cass, in frustration, accuses him of not thinking of others, when he wanders off or demands a painful artifact from the past. Is he perhaps a mix, like most of us, of the two aspects?

3. Why do you suppose the setting is left vague? We do have clues to the era, from current events discussed. And the settings of home, summer place, school, and playground are described in detail. But where we are is ambiguous. Is it perhaps to leave the story as a kind of fable, with truths for all times? Might the compression of the action in one year, with flashbacks, add to this mythic quality?

4. What do we know about the interior lives of characters other than Sebby? We can deduce attitudes and feelings, but it is all through what filter? Do the family members seem unusually bound to home? Why might that be?

5. What do you recall about food in the book? How is it important for sustaining family life or marking occasions? Often Sebby is plain not hungry. Is this a sign of his sadness? Need for control? When is a time he gobbles joyously? Is it telling that the story ends with a feast?

6. Does Sebby seem to have special dispensation just to be himself? Is he perhaps more privileged, sometimes to his peril, than other eight-year-olds who need to learn protective coloration?

7. Sebby is special, no question. What is it he provides in his near-mythic role, to other people? Challenge? Clarity? If so, what kind?

8. How does Sebby show his willingness to risk as he reaches out to others? Ms. Lambert? Jackson and Shelly? Others?

9. How does Jackson's mother provide a life line to Sebby? Are you surprised she is as non-judgmental (of both Sebby and his father) as she is?

10. How are we to understand Sebby's plunge into the water? Is it all impelled by his memory of his mother and her soap owl? Can his need to reconnect with his mother go this far?

11. We know that multicultural writing explores what it feels like to be on the edge or outside. How does this story open out into other kinds of marginality? Are we moved to remember times we have felt "other"? How do stories help us find out who we are?

12. What is the function of Sebby's letter writing to his teacher? How did you respond to those letters? What do you think they meant to Ms. Lambert? How had Sebby earlier expressed himself in heartfelt notes? Do the letters offer an important counterpoint to the rest of the narration?

13. At one point Dad says, "We still have to be a family" (p. 317). Even though the mother is said to have "left," how does she provide an enduring legacy?

14. Are you struck that Cass and Leo are truly competent, both at school and at home? Is it their necessity to function without a mother that matures them? Is it their relationship to Sebby? How do they relate to their father?

15. What is the role of world news in the novel? How does Cass particularly try to engage her family in a world beyond their own? Talk about her father's response at the end when Cass asks, "You know about Somalia?" (p. 293).

16. What are some of the precarious mental states in the book? What are the manifestations? Is there a symbolic connection between hiding under tables and beds and wandering out into the night?

17. Pictures are a central image throughout the book. Cite examples. The grandfather? The mother? Ms. Lambert? The Polaroid camera? How do pictures provide both a solace and a hope for the future for Sebby?

18. How is music important to this family? Are you familiar with the songs that provide a framework of memory for the father—and by extension for his children? Is music actually one of the ways they become a family?

19. How are books central to the lives of these children? The town library is a refuge at times. When? Do you think that Sebby's love of reading reassures the social worker? What is the father's connection with books? (see p. 66)

20. When do serious health threats afflict the family? Recall the events imperiling Sebby. And what do Dad's numb, bloody feet indicate about him? And Sebby's near frostbite?

21. What does the title mean? (see p. 25). How has Sebby held onto the concept of "up high in the trees"? Could it imply something about Sebby's special vantage point in the story?

22. Talk about Sebby's view of time in the tale. When does he want to accelerate it? Slow it down? Retrieve lost time? How does the dark hiding place at the end change from earlier hiding places? How has Sebby's idea of time evolved?

23. Even though the book often focuses on loss, specific as well as elemental, how is it also about restoration and redemption? How do love and patience, loyalty and courage work their magic?

24. What do you predict for the family in the future?

SUGGESTIONS FOR FURTHER READING:

The Ice Palace by Tarjei Vesaas; *Speak, Memory* by Vladimir Nabokov; *A Slant of Sun: One Child's Courage* by Beth Kephart; *The Year of Magical Thinking* by Joan Didion; *Childhood and Other Neighborhoods: Stories* by Stuart Dybek; *The Pink Institution* by Selah Saterstrom; *The Street of Crocodiles* by Bruno Schulz; *Hotel World* by Ali Smith; *A Portrait of the Artist as a Young Man* by James Joyce; *Monkeys* by Susan Minot; *Call It Sleep* by Henry Roth; *The Sound and the Fury* by William Faulkner; *Autobiography of Red* by Anne Carson; *Florida* by Christine Schutt; *The Collected Prose* by Elizabeth Bishop; *Running in the Family* by Michael Ondaatje; *The Question of Bruno* by Aleksandar Hemon; *Things You Should Know* by A. M. Homes; *Riddley Walker* by Russell Hoban; *Reasons to Live* by Amy Hempel